"Authentic. . . . Van Gieson's dialogue is on target; she has mastered the vernacular. Her characters . . . are well rounded and intriguing. She shows her deftness at manipulating situations and leaving the reader guessing. . . . She proves again that she is knowledgeable with her location of choice."

—*Albuquerque Journal*

Hotshots

"Van Gieson's prose is clean and refreshingly straightforward, and she has succeeded in making both her protagonist-narrator and the New Mexican locales memorable."

—*Los Angeles Times Book Review*

"Exciting. . . . We were struck with how graceful and fluid [Van Gieson's] writing has become, how skillfully she nudges along the intriguing relationship between Neil and the Kid, and how seamlessly she integrates topical issues with suspenseful storytelling."

—*Denver Post*

Parrot Blues

"Van Gieson writes with grace, tangles her phrases skillfully, and plots a compelling story down to the intricate final turns."

—*Washington Post Book World*

"A clever, winning tale."

—*Publishers Weekly*

The Lies That Bind

"Neil Hamel is funny, sexy, and very bright. . . . The detective work is excellent and well told. . . . The writing is crisp and wry."

—*Boston Globe*

"The most down-to-earth, sarcastic, anti-social, yet compassionate female protagonist on the murder mystery market today."

—*The Independent* (Gallup, NM)

The Wolf Path

"Crisp, taut, and utterly compelling."

—*Entertainment Weekly*

"Van Gieson can stand up with what the best women writers in the field have to offer."

—*Denver Post*

"[Van Gieson] and Hamel are not only in the right business, they're practicing it on the right turf."

—*Detroit News*

BY JUDITH VAN GIESON

Ditch Rider
Hotshots
Parrot Blues
The Lies That Bind
The Wolf Path
The Other Side of Death
Raptor
North of the Border

JUDITH VAN GIESON

DITCH RIDER

A NEIL HAMEL MYSTERY

HarperPaperbacks
A Division of HarperCollinsPublishers

HarperPaperbacks
A Division of HarperCollins*Publishers*
10 East 53rd Street, New York, NY 10022-5299

This is a work of fiction. The characters, incidents, and dialogues
are products of the author's imagination and are not to be
construed as real. Any resemblance to actual events or persons,
living or dead, is entirely coincidental.

Visit HarperPaperbacks on the World Wide Web at
http://www.harpercollins.com

❖ 10 9 8 7 6 5 4 3 2 1

This book is dedicated to
attorney Alan M. Uris,
my old friend and legal adviser,
and to the girls and the boy in my hood

ACKNOWLEDGMENTS

Thanks to Paige, Marisela, Liz, Nedia, Sharon, Michelle, Jessica, Tony and Emilio. I couldn't have written this book without you.

1

I have the only house on Mirador Road with a courtyard. It's my buffer between the living room and the street. My neighbors live in cinderblock houses and trailers; their only buffers are the cars and trucks parked in their scraped-bare yards. In my hood the smaller the house the greater the number of vehicles parked in front of it. The neighbors have chain-link fences and an occasional rosebush or plum tree. I have a weed that grew into a Siberian elm and shades my courtyard in summer. In the winter the bare branches mark time on the wall with their shadows. My courtyard has a *banco* (an adobe bench) growing

out of the wall, a brick floor and a struggling rosebush planted by a previous owner. The adobe wall
snakes across a wooden door that has a chevron pattern to the boards. There's enough space between the
V's to see the outline of who's coming, but not the
details. When the bell rings, it can be someone trying to sell me black-market t-shirts or just checking
to see if anyone's home. Or else it's Jehovah's Witnesses and Mormons on the conversion trail. This
time it was a small person with a halo of blonde
hair.

"Who's there?" I asked before flipping the latch.

"Cheyanne."

She sounded harmless, so I opened the door. My
visitor had a mane of blonde curls pulled high above
her head and tumbling down her back. She wore
shorts and an extra-large Chicago Bulls t-shirt. Her
skin was the color of vanilla ice cream, something
you notice in my neighborhood. Her fingernails were
painted blue, her lipstick was black. She held a candy
bar in one hand. The other hand cradled a baby
wrapped in a blanket.

"I'm selling candy for my school," she said,
showing me the candy bar. Her nails were bitten
down and there was white space at the cuticle where
the blue had grown out. "WORLD'S FINEST CHOCO-
LATE," the candy bar wrapper read. "FUND RAIS-
ERS—THANK YOU FOR YOUR SUPPORT." Behind the

girl a boy on a bike pedaled slowly down the street.

"How much?" I asked her.

"A dollar."

"A dollar for that?" The candy bar was no wider than two pencils, no longer than Cheyanne's finger.

She shrugged. "It's for the school."

"What school?"

"Taylor Middle."

"All right. I'll take two." One for me. One for my live-in lover, the Kid. "Come on in. I'll get you the money."

She kicked the door shut behind her, followed me across the courtyard and into the living room looking around at my beehive-shaped adobe fireplace and at the vigas in my ceiling. I went in search of my purse.

"Baaad house," she said when I came back with the money.

"Thanks." I gave her two dollars. She gave me two candy bars. "Where do you live?" I asked.

"In the double-wide down the street. You have a computer?"

She'd noticed the Equus that the Kid, a mechanic, had taken in trade for fixing somebody's truck. I'd been trying to do research for my law practice when Cheyanne rang the doorbell. "Yeah."

The surf box was on the screen. "You're on the Internet. Cool. My girlfriend's dad has a computer but he won't let her on the Internet. He says she'll cost him too much money."

"I was trying to use it for work myself."

"Whatta you do?"

"I'm a lawyer."

"Downtown, right?"

"How'd you know?"

"I see you go by in the morning." She stared at the computer. Her fingers seemed hungry for the keyboard like a musician's drawn to the sax or piano. "Would you mind . . . ?"

"Go ahead," I said.

She put the baby down on the sofa.

"Boy or girl?" I asked.

"Girl. Her name is Miranda."

She sat down at the computer. Her fingernails skipped across the keys and pulled Teen Chat up on the screen. "Any *hueros* out there?" she typed, sending her message onto the information highway.

"You know what *hueros* are?" she asked.

"White dudes," I said.

"Right." She laughed. "You, me and my mom, we're the only *hueras* who live on this block. Did you know that?"

I'd suspected, but I hadn't actually known. Leave it to the kids to know who everybody was in the hood.

"That's a fine guy you got living here. He reminds me of Carlos Leon."

"Who's that?"

"The dude Madonna's had a baby with."

Older, younger, lighter, darker. As far as I was concerned, that was where any resemblance to Carlos and Madonna ended. No baby on my horizon. No big bucks or personal trainers, either.

The private room message came up on the screen, the place one teen can talk to another privately. "What's your name?" it asked.

"Cheyanne," she typed.

"What do you look like?"

"I have blonde hair."

"How old are you?"

"Eighteen." Going on sixteen. Maybe. The baby on the sofa began to cry. Cheyanne continued to type, but the baby wasn't going to be ignored. Her cries escalated in volume. Cheyanne spun around. "Shut up, you little brat," she screamed. "Can't you see I'm having fun?" The baby couldn't see or didn't care. Cheyanne left the keyboard and stomped across the room. She lifted Miranda and held her high like she was preparing to give the baby a good, hard shake.

"Don't even consider it," I warned.

"You're right. I'd never get away with it." She unwrapped the blanket, flipped the baby onto its stomach, turned a key in its back and shut the crying off.

"That's a doll?"

"Kinda. They give us these babies in school, see. We have to feed 'em, take care of 'em when they cry, and not rough 'em up. One day they'll have one that pees, and then we'll have to change the diaper. It's got a computer inside so if we don't take care of it the teacher will know. It's supposed to make us not want a real kid."

"Is it working?"

"I guess. Some of these dolls act like babies born on drugs. They're smaller than the other babies. They cry for fifty minutes and they shake all the time. Even when you hold them they shake. They're real expensive, so we don't get to take them home."

"How old are you?" I asked.

"Thirteen."

"What grade?"

"Eighth."

Eighth grade wasn't what it used to be, and neither was thirteen. I'd thought I was bad when I was thirteen, but that was many years ago and bad isn't what it used to be either. Having taken care of Miranda's programmed needs, Cheyanne went back to the computer and found the box of Digital Schoolhouse CD's that had come with the system. I hadn't opened the box because it sounded educational.

"You have Schoolhouse!" Cheyanne said. "Cool! Would you mind?"

"Go ahead."

"You're sure? I mean, I'm not overstaying my welcome, am I? My mom says not to do that."

"I'll tell you if you do."

Cheyanne took a CD out of the box, placed it in the D drive and loaded it. The copyright information came up, tinny music played, a spider appeared in the corner of the screen and spun a web. Cheyanne sang along with the music. Her head kept time and her blonde curls bobbed. "Itsy-bitsy spider went up the waterspout." Her fingers left the keyboard and made a spider's climbing motions.

The phone rang and I answered it. It was a guy from Celestial Dry Cleaners offering me a special on upholstery and carpet cleaning.

"I don't have any upholstery and I don't have any carpets," I replied. The guy hung up.

"What time is it?" Cheyanne asked.

"Around three."

"A la! I gotta go. My mom'll kill me." She logged out of the nursery rhymes, put the CD away and picked up the bogus baby.

I walked her across the courtyard and opened the door. The boy on the bike—who was not a *huero*—had parked across the street. His hair was slick and black. He wore a t-shirt with a logo that read GOOSE-BUMPS. He had a souped-up bike, the low rider of bikes, with a polished brass chain and tassels that dangled from the handlebars.

"Cool bike," I said.

Cheyanne yelled, "Danny, you dork. Stop following me!"

The boy put his feet to the pedals, the rubber to the road and rode away with his head down and his elbows poking into the street.

When the Kid came home I told him about my visitor. "I've never seen her," he said.

Then I told him about the boy on the bike. He didn't know who Danny was, either, but he knew about the bikes. "There's a club here," he told me. "They work on the bikes like the big boys work on cars. Sometimes I fix things for them. It keeps them out of trouble, out of gangs."

"How old are the boys?"

He shrugged. "Nine. Ten."

"Isn't that a little young for gangs?"

"Not anymore. They like to rank in the little ones they call peewees. Peewees will do anything to be accepted."

"The Church used to say 'Give me a boy until he's nine and he's mine forever,'" I told him. The Kid had grown up in enough Latin American countries to know all about that Church. "Now it's give me a boy when he's that age and it's gangbang forever?"

"Yeah," the Kid said. "The boys ride their bikes along the ditches. I can see them from the back of the shop."

It would give the boys a special point of view—the backyards, the faces that people hide from the world. Everybody sees their neighborhood differently. Cheyanne had seen the Kid and I, but we hadn't noticed her. I had noticed the boy. The Kid had noticed the bikes.

"Cheyanne knows who you are. She told me a fine guy lived here." The Kid laughed. He was slightly sweaty from work and looking pretty good to me right now. "How come she knows about us and we don't know about her?"

"She's a little girl and they are home more. They have the time, you have the power. You always notice what the people with more power do."

"I have power?"

"You own a house. You work downtown."

"That's not much."

"It's enough here," the Kid said. I gave him his candy bar and watched him roll down the wrapper. What kind of power did he have? I wondered. He was tall and skinny, had thick, curly hair and could fix things. That was part of it. A guy from a middle-class Argentine family that had been forced to emigrate to Mexico, he'd taken the immigrant's route of starting his own business once he reached the U.S.A. In his journey through the Americas he'd taken a turn that led him to believe in himself. Sometimes that's power enough.

I looked out the window at the herb garden behind my house—also the work of the previous owner, who'd planted the mint, oregano, sage and catnip. All I do to keep it green is turn the drip irrigation on in the spring and off in the fall—my idea of gardening. An orange and white tabby was nibbling on the catnip and getting a fix.

2

Cheyanne started show-
ing up now and then with Miranda cradled in her arm. She liked to hang out at my house and search for guys on the computer. Whenever she asked if she'd overstayed her welcome, I said not yet. I didn't meet many teenagers in my line of life, and teen talk was a break from the adult wrangling I usually dealt with.

One Saturday Cheyanne came to the door with another girl who had the same blue fingernails and big hair, only the other girl's hair was dark and her Chicago Bulls t-shirt was an extra small. Every time the subject of having to wear school uniforms comes up in Albuquerque, teenagers complain loudly, but it looked to me like they were already wearing uni-forms—Chicago Bulls t-shirts in summer, Chicago Bulls jackets in winter.

"Hi," Cheyanne said. "This is my friend Patricia."

"Hi," I replied. "Where's Miranda?"

"Home with my mom."

"Do you have one of those bogus babies, too?" I asked Patricia.

"No way," she said.

The Kid had taken the day off and was in the driveway washing his truck.

"That's your guy out there. Right?" Cheyanne said.

"Right," I said.

"He's never here when I come over."

"He works a lot."

"Can we meet him?" Patricia asked, looking up at me from under heavily made-up eyelids.

"Come on in." They followed me inside.

"Baaad house, huh?" Cheyanne said to Patricia.

"Real baaad," Patricia agreed.

I'd mastered the CD-ROM and Radio Austin was playing on the D drive. The girls started gig-gling, line dancing and doing a wicked imitation of a big-haired country-western singer. They mouthed the words, snapped their fingers, shook their tousled heads.

I went out back to round up the Kid, which took

a few minutes because he wanted to get the soap off the truck before the sun baked it in place. The music had stopped and Cheyanne was showing Patricia Digital Schoolhouse when we returned.

"That stuff's for children," Patricia said.

"I play the music for Miranda. She likes it." Cheyanne laughed.

"She's not a real baby, you know."

"I know." Cheyanne's laugh turned into a pout. Her moods changed as fast as the weather did on cloud cam.

"You stole that doll from the school."

"I didn't steal it. I only borrowed it for a few days."

"A few months, you mean. What's gonna happen when they catch you?"

"They're not gonna catch me."

I broke up the quarrel and introduced the Kid.

"That's your shop on Fourth Street, right?" Patricia asked. "The one with the flying red horse sign outside?"

"Right."

"I hear you have a parrot there."

"Yeah."

"What's its name?"

"Mimo."

"Does it talk?"

"*Mas o menos.*" He shrugged. "It says hello and *pendejo.*"

It said *pendejo* (asshole) a lot more than it said hello. Mimo liked the reaction it got to *pendejo*. Patricia laughed, then lowered her lids and looked at her blue nails. "There was a shooting over by there last night," she said. "In the strip mall on Ladera. Did you know that?"

The Kid shook his head. "No."

"A guy named Juan Padilla was killed."

"I don't know him."

"How old was he?" I asked.

"Fifteen," said Patricia.

"How did it happen?" asked the Kid.

Cheyanne had been tugging the tail of her t-shirt and doing a little dance while Patricia told the Kid about the death of Juan Padilla. There was something she wanted to say and she'd been waiting for the chance to say it. She planted her feet, let go of her t-shirt and blurted it out. "It was like this, see. Juan and this other guy, they had a fight. They weren't brothers exactly but they were like that. Juan got scared and he pulled a gun. He didn't want to shoot the other guy, he was just scared, but the other guy didn't know that, see, so he shot Juan first."

"Did you know Juan?" I asked her.

"He went to Valley High. I didn't really know him."

"That's not the way it happened," Patricia put her two cents in. "It was gang shit. Juan dissed some-

DITCH RIDER ◆ 15

body and he got offed for it. It was a power play. The guy that shot him was showing his colors, making his name come out. That's what really happened."

"Which gang?" I asked.

"What difference does it make?" Patricia flipped her hair over her shoulder. "They're all the same. No matter what color they carry, they all bleed red."

"It could make a difference to the APD."

"Anybody who killed Juan will be dead before they get him," Patricia said.

She had a point. Gang justice was swifter and more effective than the APD's.

"It didn't happen the way you said," Patricia told Cheyanne. "Those guys were nothing like brothers."

"Maybe they were alike on the inside. Everybody wants the same things, right?"

"Or they want somebody else's things."

"I guess," Cheyanne said in a small voice.

"Are you thirteen, too?" I asked the world-weary Patricia.

"Fifteen in December," she said. "I'm in high school, but Cheyanne and me, we've been friends for a long time from when she used to live on my street." They were close in chronological age, but Cheyanne had a few months of childhood left and Patricia appeared to have none, the effect, maybe, of high school. Patricia started as if she'd been stung by a bee, then she pulled a beeper out of her pocket. "It's my mom. We have to use the ones that vibrate now," she explained, "because of school. They take them away if they beep and you don't get them back till school's out."

I was standing close enough to see the numbers that had come up on the beeper, 303. "How do you know it's your mom?" I asked.

"If you turn the three over it looks like an M, see? M O M."

"Oh, yeah."

Patricia punched Cheyanne in the shoulder. "Gotta go, girl."

"Nice to meet you," Cheyanne said to the Kid.

"Mucho gusto," he replied.

"El gusto es mio," said Patricia, looking up at the Kid with lazy eyes.

The minute the girls were across the courtyard and out the door he said, *"Estas vatas estan corriendo sin aceite."* Those girls are running without oil.

"An accident waiting to happen," I replied. "What do you think they wanted?"

"To tell me about Juan Padilla."

"Why you?" Because he was the only man available that day in the hood?

"The little one is scared. The big one? I don't know."

"There's no little one and big one. Those girls are the same size."

"The one with the dark hair is bigger, no?"

"Older, not bigger. She was flirting with you. Did you notice?"

If he had, he wouldn't admit it. "She's a little girl," he said, "she doesn't know what she's doing." He turned and walked toward the back of the house where his truck baked in the sun.

I let him go, went out to the courtyard and sat down on the *banco*. The wall vibrated as a stereo on wheels pounded by. A lullaby tinkled when the ice-cream truck showed up. Pigeons perching on the electric line fluttered and cooed.

In the morning the Kid and I followed the Chapuzar Lateral to Casa de Benavidez Restaurant. The neighborhood I live in is crisscrossed with laterals, wasteways, ditches, canals, *acequias* and drains. They are the arteries and veins that carry Rio Grande water through a valley that has been irrigated for 900 years at least. There are roads beside the ditches that are supposed to be used for maintenance. They are not a legal access, but that doesn't stop anyone from using them. Albuquerque has a lawless past it never wants to forget. In some places there are no roads beside the ditches—only footpaths. You can ride or walk all over the valley on the paths.

The Chapuzar Lateral is a major north-south artery with a road on the west side and a footpath on the east. We took the footpath, stepping on the hieroglyphics left by horseshoes, running shoes and mountain bike wheels. If you knew how to cut sign, they'd tell you who had been here and when. Weeds grew tall on the ditch banks, and the intense green contrasted nicely with the Sandia Mountains' distant blue. Pink and white wild morning glories wrapped their tendrils around the weeds. The vegetation hid the cross streets in front of and behind us and made it appear that we were following a long country road. The cottonwoods that grew here had trunks thick enough to support several treehouses. Their branches wandered across the paths dropping cotton that the wind whipped into a whirling dervish. The ditches were high today; somewhere to the north someone had lifted a board to let the brown muddy water flow.

"They call the people who maintain the ditches Ditch Riders, did you know that?" I asked the Kid.

"No."

"They take care of the cleaning and the weeding. They try to keep people from falling in. They set the irrigation schedules and settle the arguments." But there were probably fewer arguments these days than there used to be because the alfalfa fields and horse pastures in the valley were being replaced by subdivisions, and people in subdivisions don't bother with water that comes from the ditch.

At the place where a culvert guided the flow under Montera Street, the trash had backed up. Plastic bottles bobbed in the water, and I saw the twisted white belly of a dead snake. A pheasant with a red eye and a ring around its neck ran down the path and darted into a field. A mallard flapped its wings and lifted out of the water. The ditches are the valley's watering hole, the place wildlife comes to drink and eat—or get eaten. At night the predators and La Llorona take over. La Llorona is a legend in New Mexico, a tale parents tell to warn their children away from trouble. The legend differs from town to town. In some places she's drowned her own children and the current runs red with their blood. In others she haunts the ditch banks, searching for her lost children with the red eyes of an owl. Sometimes she floats like a canoe on the water. Wherever she is and whatever she does, she's crying.

There was a dead hawk on the path. What could kill a hawk around here but a coyote? I wondered. I've never seen a coyote in the valley, but they frequent other parts of town. I turned and looked back at my house. From this angle it seemed sheltered by its courtyard and high wooden fence.

We crossed over a few more streets, passed

behind the Kid's shop and came to Ladera. From here we could see the strip mall where Juan Padilla had been shot. The police tape marked the site as being behind the mall, which meant the body could have laid there for hours before it was discovered.

When we reached Casa de Benavidez I stopped to buy the Sunday *Journal* at the vending machine. The Kid went inside and sat down at a table on the patio. A waterfall splashed into a pond that had water lilies floating on top and orange carp swimming underneath. A sign warned parents to keep their children away from the pool, but a barefoot little girl in her pink Sunday best tiptoed along the edge singing to herself. She turned around, saw her parents weren't watching and dipped her foot in the water.

"What are you going to have?" the Kid asked me.

"Papas, bacon, OJ, coffee," I said. I didn't ask him what he wanted; I knew it would be his favorite breakfast food, a chicharrones burrito. Chicharrones (aka fried fat) weren't something I wanted to face this early in the day, so I unfolded the paper. Juan Padilla's murder was on page one. A witness described the shooter as a gang member, an Anglo teenager, sixteen or seventeen years old, six feet tall with a slender build, curly blonde hair and an earring in one ear. The police were working up a sketch. The body hadn't been found until 2:00 A.M.—too late for the Saturday *Journal*. Crimestoppers was offering a reward, and the witness would get it if the shooter and the description matched. The case was likely to be handled by my buddy in the District Attorney's office, Deputy DA Anthony Saia, who'd been put in charge of gang violence. Some details of the crime were revealed; some were not. The APD can't give away too much or the DA will never get a conviction.

The Kid bit into his burrito and the chicharrones crunched. I ate my bacon. The little girl's parents told her to get away from the water, waking her from her dream. Her foot dipped into the pool and the water splashed all over her pink dress.

"Juan Padilla's body was found at two A.M. yesterday morning," I told the Kid. "A witness said it was gang-related and the shooter was a white teenager around six feet tall."

"Gangs," the Kid said. "The big girl was right about that."

"Are there gangs in this neighborhood?" I asked him. I hadn't seen the telltale signs, like graffiti tags all over the walls, pants that went beyond baggy or the t-shirts with Old English letters and comedy and tragedy masks that gang members wear to mourn their dead.

"Sure. They have cars. They can go everywhere. They can go to any high school they want to—if they want to go to school. If they go to the D Home or prison they teach everybody else what they know. It's *LaVida Loca*, the crazy life. Sometimes I fix their cars for them."

"What are they like?"

"Don't worry about them, *chiquita*. They go after each other, not us."

I was interested in how gangs had co-opted the symbols of another time and place, the way Elizabethan England had resurfaced in twentieth-century Albuquerque. "Those masks they wear on their t-shirts are the faces of comedy and tragedy," I said. "What does that mean to them?"

"Smile now, cry later," he said.

3

On Monday the police sketch appeared in the *Journal*. The suspect had a thin face with high cheekbones, a long, straight nose, narrow eyes. He had curly blonde hair and wore an earring in one ear. What distinguished him from your average white dude was an expression of total malice.

"I wouldn't want to run into him in a parking lot at night," my secretary Anna said when I showed her the picture.

"Me neither."

"How old, do they think?"

"Sixteen or seventeen."

Anna studied the sketch. "He wouldn't be bad

looking if he wasn't giving somebody the stinkeye."

He did have the even features that pass for good looks in our society. "He was shooting a fifteen-year-old boy when the witness saw him. Maybe the sketch artist was trying to recapture the moment."

"If he looked like that all the time he should have been locked up long ago," Anna said.

It turned out that the suspect had been arrested several times, but he was Teflon-coated—none of the charges had stuck. On Tuesday, his name, Ron Cade, appeared in the paper. The police said he was a member of a Heights gang. By now they had a photo and the *Journal* ran it. The witness had given the police a near-perfect description of the perp. The photo was very close to the sketch, except that Ron Cade's lips had a ripple of a smile in the photo. As might be expected, he hadn't been seen since the shooting. Ron Cade might have run away to live out his life in Mexico or California, or he might already be dead and rotting somewhere on a mesa or in a ditch.

I got home around seven that evening. It had been a boring day, and I'd spent most of it in my office pushing paper. The ice-cream truck was parked on Mirador, and some bike riders were gathered around it eating Popsicles. I waved to them as I drove by. It was one of those summer evenings when even the leaves on the trees are still. A field full of alfalfa in the middle of the block had been cut and baled as tight as tombstones. The sun had reached the place where it lingers before beginning its final descent. It was beating into the west side of my house and turning it hotter than a car that's been parked at the mall all day. I figured the Kid wouldn't be home until dark. I could have called him, but it was cooler outside than it was in, so I decided to walk down the ditch and ask him what he wanted to do about dinner.

When I got to the shop he was working on a 1950s Chevy, one of those classic cars he calls Fast Fives. The owner was hanging around waiting for the Kid to finish up. The guy's head was clipped and narrow. He wore wide, knee-length pants with boxer shorts sticking out over the waistband, knee socks and sandals. The short full pants reminded me of the culottes women used to wear. We've come to a weird place, I thought, where guys act tough by dressing like 1950s women. The Kid finished up. The guy thanked him, paid him in cash and drove away.

"Gangbanger?" I asked.

"Yeah," the Kid replied.

"Which one?"

"The Fourth Street Originals. That was Juan Padilla's gang. Everybody calls them the Four O's, but I call them the *feos*." The uglies.

"He was pretty ugly."

"Some gangs like drugs and violence. Some just like violence. The Four O's are violent. Some of them are *bajo cero* . . ."

Below zero.

". . . but some of them are not too bad."

"Why do they always wear gray and black?" I asked.

"The Nortenos' colors are red, the Sudenos' are blue. If anybody else wears those colors they get in trouble, so these guys just wear gray and black." The Kid shook his head. "They know all about guns, but they know nothing about cars. They can't fix anything."

"I think their role is breaking, not fixing."

"*Verdad*," said the Kid.

"What do you want for dinner?" I asked.

"Lota Burger?"

"Okay."

"I'll get them when I finish here," he said.

I lingered in the shop trying to teach Mimo another word. I was working on good-bye, but Mimo was a stubborn bird. I think it knew the words, it just didn't feel like saying them.

"Try *adios*," said the Kid. That didn't work either. Finally I gave up, put the hood over its cage and put the parrot to bed.

★   ★   ★

When I started back home the sun had taken a dive, leaving behind a green afterglow in the west and turning the jet trails above the Sandias into golden squiggles. The cicadas were screaming their late summer song. The water in the ditch had a smooth, dark shimmer. A train wailed from the tracks near Rosa. In the fading light it was hard to tell where the trees ended and the shadows began. I picked up my pace, listening to the water lapping gently at the ditch banks. There was a rustling in the field beside me that might have been a skunk or a dog, but I could see two of them and one of them wore a white shirt. Kids getting it on beside the ditch. I hesitated, but kept on walking. I wasn't a parent. I wasn't the police. I'd been a reckless teen once myself.

"Don't!" A girl's voice squealed like a small, frightened animal.

"What's happening?" I called. If they were getting it on, it was without the girl's consent. There wasn't a whole lot I could do about it without a weapon, but that didn't stop me from trying.

"Leave me alone!" the girl yelled.

"Chill, bitch," a guy said. He stood up and stared at me long enough to tell that he was tall, blonde, thin, wearing a white t-shirt and wide pants. He walked across the field and disappeared into the shadows.

The girl who climbed up onto the ditch bank

was Cheyanne. "Are you all right?" I asked her.

"Yeah," she said, but she shivered while I walked her back to my house.

I led her into the courtyard and locked the door behind us. Under the sensor light that comes on at dusk, I could see that she was dressed in shorts and a t-shirt, that her clothes were dirty and mussed but not bloody or torn, that her hair had come loose and was falling down around her face.

"Was that guy trying to rape you?" I asked.

She shook her head.

"What did he want?"

"I don't know."

"Cheyanne, a guy's beating you up beside the ditch and you don't know what he wants?" If she'd been carrying anything he could have stolen, it was long gone.

"It was nothing," she said, her face turning sullen.

"Was it Ron Cade?"

"I don't know who it was. Just some guy."

"Do you want me to walk you home? Do you want me to call your mother?"

"No. Could I wash my face before I go home?"

"Okay," I said.

We went into the house, and while the water was running in the bathroom I went into the kitchen and called the Kid. He was somewhere between Lota

Burger and home, and he didn't carry a cell phone in his pocket or truck. When Cheyanne came out of the bathroom, her hair was slicked back and her face was clean. She walked down the hallway and caught up with me in the kitchen. There was a basket of fruit on the counter and her hand latched onto a mango.

"What's this?" she asked me.

"A mango."

"Can I have it?"

"Sure."

She took the mango and said she had to go. She insisted on walking home alone, but she couldn't stop me from standing outside my doorway and watching her do it. When we went outside we could see that the moon had risen and clouds were settling into a saddle of the Sandias as if they were filling an empty cup.

"The sky is falling," Cheyanne said.

I watched her walk down the street and waited until she'd entered the trailer and shut the door behind her.

A few minutes later the Kid showed up. When I told him what had happened he drove around the hood in his truck, but he didn't see signs of Ron Cade or of anyone else who looked like trouble.

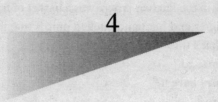

4

A few days later when the doorbell rang at eight in the morning, I was in the kitchen drinking coffee and the Kid had left for work. It was too early to have my guard up, so I lifted the latch without bothering to ask who'd come calling. A small, tense woman stood before me. Her hair was thin and brassy from too much bleach. Her skin was weathered from too much sun. Her eyes were a pale, weary brown. She wore silver filigree earrings, a miniskirt, high heels and a green t-shirt with a Sandia Indian Bingo logo. She was smoking a cigarette that even at eight in the morning I coveted.

She coughed and cleared her throat. "Are you the

lawyer?" she asked in a smoker's raspy voice. Smokers are often drinkers, and I wondered what this woman's drink might be. Not beer. She didn't have the subcutaneous layer of flab.

"My name is Neil Hamel," I said. *And this is my home, not my office,* I thought.

"I'm Sonia. Sonia Moran." She took another drag on her cigarette, blowing some smoke in my direction. "I live down the street in the trailer. Cheyanne's my daughter. Can I come in?"

"Okay."

She followed me across the courtyard, and when she got to the front door she stopped and stared at her half-burned butt. "You want me to throw this away? I know some people don't like it when you smoke in their houses."

I wouldn't want to be known as a person who ran a no-smoking household. It hadn't been that long ago that I'd smoked in this house myself. "Actually, your cigarette looks pretty good and I am trying to quit."

"I can understand that," she said. "I've quit many times myself." She took a deep drag, dropped the cigarette on the brick floor and ground it out. We went into the living room and sat down on the sofa.

"Would you like some coffee?" I asked.

"No thanks. I'm getting ready to go to bed. I

worked late—I'm a blackjack dealer at Sandia—and then I was up all night waiting for my goddamned daughter to come home."

"Cheyanne didn't come home last night?"

"Not till five in the morning she didn't."

I wondered if I ought to tell Sonia about finding her daughter beside the ditch, but I decided to see what Sonia had to say first. There's a law that says doctors can't tell a mother when a daughter is pregnant. Maybe there was another law that says a lawyer ought to keep a daughter's secrets.

"Fucking police," Sonia said. "There's supposed to be a curfew in this town. Why the hell are they letting teenagers stay out all night anyway?"

Which could be exactly what the police were saying about the parents. "There are more teenagers than there are police, and at five in the morning the teenagers have more energy," I said. "What is it you wanted to talk to me about?" I did have an office to get to.

"You know Juan Padilla? The boy that got shot?"

"Yeah."

"When Cheyanne finally got home this morning she told me she was the one that shot him."

That was the kind of news that could shatter your life.

"She says she pulled the trigger."

"Do you believe her?"

"That's what she says."

"Where's the weapon? Does she have it?"

"She told me she threw it in the ditch."

"Did she tell you what kind of gun it was?"

"A thirty-eight, she says."

"A thirty-eight?" Tech Nines were the guns of choice in gang slayings. Even a thirteen-year-old was likely to know that.

"Yeah."

"How did the shooting happen?"

"She says she was with some guys and there was an argument. She was holding the gun for one of them. She says she didn't mean to kill Juan, but the gun went off."

"What guys?"

"She's too scared to tell."

That made sense in New Mexico. "We have a law in this state that makes an accessory as guilty as the shooter."

"Yeah? I didn't know that," Sonia said. She was rubbing her fingers together—the telltale gesture of a worrier in need of a bead or a smoker in need of a butt.

I wondered how much Cheyanne knew about the accessory law and, if so, who had told her. Gangs, I figured, would have their own accessory laws.

Sonia fixed her tired eyes on me. "Could you help us?" she pleaded. "Cheyanne thinks a lot of you.

I know you could represent her better than anybody, but I can't afford to pay you much."

"Don't worry about it," I said. "If I take the case, we'll work something out."

"Maybe I'll win the lottery."

"Maybe."

Her eyes filled up with tears. "Is Cheyanne gonna spend the rest of her life in prison for this?"

It was a parent's second-worst nightmare. The first is that her own child will be lying dead in the street.

"She don't know nothing 'bout guns. She didn't mean to kill Juan. She was hangin' with the wrong people, that's all. It was just a dumb mistake."

Dumb for her, maybe, fatal for Juan, a nightmare for his family and friends. "Cheyanne is thirteen, isn't she?"

"That's right."

"All the state can do to a thirteen-year-old is put her in the Girls' School for two years." Prosecutors had tried to get consecutive two-year terms, but no one had succeeded yet. Two years was the maximum under our justice system, but it was unlikely gang members would be so willing to forgive and forget.

"Really?" Her sense of relief was so strong that for a minute her fingers stopped fidgeting and she forgot how much she needed a cigarette.

"Really. Did Cheyanne know Juan Padilla?"

"He used to hang out around the place some, but

when he got in a gang I told him I didn't want him comin' around no more. I don't want gangs rankin' in my boy, Danny. Look, I gotta go back to work this afternoon. I need to get some sleep, and I'll sleep a whole lot better if you'll just tell me you'll represent Cheyanne."

"She hasn't been charged with anything yet," I pointed out. "A witness fingered a guy named Ron Cade, who's a member of a Heights gang. The police are looking for him. Did he hang out around the place, too?"

"Not as far as I know."

"The shooting happened Friday night. Do you know where Cheyanne was then?"

She shook her head. "I was working."

"And after work?"

"I went to see my boyfriend. Will you help us? Please. Cheyanne'll be better off in the Girls' School for two years than she will on the street. My boy's always been good as can be, but I never could do nothin' with her."

"I need to talk to Cheyanne before I make a decision."

Sonia stood up. "I'll go get her."

"I need to talk to her alone," I said.

"You think she's gonna tell you something she didn't tell me?"

"She might."

"She's my daughter," Sonia insisted.

"She'll be my client," I replied.

"You lawyerin' me?"

"Just doing my job," I said.

Sonia was too tired to argue. "All right." The minute she was out of the house she lit up, Marlboro Reds. If she was a drinker I figured her for Jack Daniel's, a smooth, cool, seductive drink, a gambler's drink, a drink that tasted good. Jack Daniel's could make you believe it would make things better. My preference, Cuervo Gold, didn't taste good enough to make any promises. All it offered and all it delivered was to kill the pain. I opened the street door for Sonia and saw Danny waiting on his souped-up bike.

"Hi, darlin'." Sonia gave him a hug with one hand and tousled his hair with the other, leaving the cigarette to dangle from her lip. "You're on your way to school?"

He nodded.

"Do me a favor, will you, and get your sister."

"Okay." Danny pedaled away on his bike.

"That's my good kid," Sonia said while Danny was still within earshot. "My nine-year-old."

Good kid. Bad kid. Some roles are assigned early, and once they are it's hard not to live up to them. I knew that because I'd been the bad kid myself. "Danny's Cheyanne's brother?" I asked.

"Half brother. They have different fathers. You

know how that is. Danny's father's Hispanic. Cheyanne says you have a Hispanic guy living here."

"Yeah."

"Mexican men can be rough, but they can be
kind, too, if you know what I mean."

Actually, I did. "He's not Mexican. He was born
in Argentina."

"Well, he speaks Spanish, right?"

"Right."

"Spanish guys in this country get treated like
women, so they know how that feels. It can make
them gentle if it don't make them mean. Cheyanne's
father was a mean son of a bitch. He was gone before
she was even out of the womb. But Danny's father,
he keeps in touch. He works, gives me money for
Danny. He does things with his boy and he'd do 'em
with Cheyanne too if she'd let him. Cheyanne likes
to think her father is an Indian. Does she look like
she has any Indian blood to you?"

"No."

"She gave herself the name Cheyanne, but she
spells it C-H-E-Y-A-N-N-E. She always did have a
lot of imagination."

"What's her real name?"

"Charlene."

Charlene/Cheyanne was following Danny down
the street looking rumpled and tired. She cradled the
fat orange and white cat in her arms.

"Neil here wants to talk to you alone," Sonia said.

"Can I bring Tabatoe in?"

"No, you cannot! Put that damn cat down."

Cheyanne put Tabatoe on the ground, and the cat made a dash for the catnip patch.

"You tell Neil everything. You hear me?" Sonia said.

"I hear you," Cheyanne mumbled to her running shoe.

"What?"

"I HEAR YOU!" Like many conversations between mothers and daughters, this one was full of capital letters and exclamation points.

"All right." Sonia turned around and walked home with her high heels tapping the street. Danny rode his bike toward school. I led Cheyanne into the house, called my office and told Anna I'd be late. Cheyanne would be late for school herself, but under the circumstances that didn't seem critical. In fact, it seemed wiser not to go. The best thing for Cheyanne at this point would be to stay home and barricade the door or to get out of town if she had a father or anybody else to go to.

First I asked her why she went out last night. "Nobody was home. Danny was with his father. I was lonely," she said.

"Where did you go?"

"To Patricia's house."

"That was Ron Cade you were with when I saw you beside the ditch, wasn't it?"

She nodded.

"Will you tell me what happened with him?"

"Nothing. He tried to rough me up is all, but I curled up in a ball and pretended I was a little animal, see. He didn't hurt me. It was no big deal."

"Did you see him again last night? Did he convince you to confess to Juan Padilla's killing in order to cover for him? They can't do much to you, but they could put him away for life."

"It wasn't like that."

"Why did you tell your mother about Juan this morning?"

"I couldn't keep it a secret no more. You're not going to tell my mom about Ron Cade, are you?"

"It would be better if she knew."

"Don't tell her, please. She'll kill me."

"I can't represent you, Cheyanne, if you're not honest with me."

"I'm honest." Not exactly. If nothing else, there were lies of omission.

"Were you with Ron the night Juan was killed?"

"Anybody I was with is as guilty as me, right?"

"Probably."

"Then don't make me tell you that." She squirmed in her chair.

"I'm your lawyer, not your judge. Whatever you say stops here."

"I can't," she mumbled.

Who were you with? was a question you might not want to ask an adult client. And there was a real good chance you'd never ask my next question; sometimes it's better not to know. But this client was only thirteen years old. I tried to get her to look me in the eye, but her eyes were fixed on her big toe. "Did you shoot Juan Padilla?" I asked her.

"I didn't mean to," she mumbled.

"I didn't ask whether you meant to. I asked if you did."

She nodded.

"Don't nod. We're talking about murder here. Maybe Juan wasn't an altar boy, but he was a person. He had a family, he had a life, he had dreams just like you."

"I know," she said. Tears were running down her face.

"I want an answer and I want you to look at me when you give it. Did you shoot Juan Padilla?"

She raised her eyes, and although she looked harder at the wall than she did at me, she gave me an answer. "Yes. I shot Juan Padilla. All right?"

"No," I said. "It's not all right, but I'll do what I can to help you."

"Thank you," she whispered.

"How many times did you pull the trigger?"

"Only once. It was an accident, like I said. I wasn't trying to kill nobody."

"Where did the bullet hit Juan?"

"In the heart." She put her hands to her chest to show me the spot.

"What kind of gun was it?"

"A thirty-eight."

"Where'd you get it?"

"I can't tell you that."

"Wait here a minute." I went and got my own Ladysmith thirty-eight, which—at the moment—was residing unloaded in my bedside table. I checked to be sure—no bullets—and handed the gun to Cheyanne. "Show me how it happened," I said.

She stared at the gun as if it were a centipede, curled, angry and ready to bite.

"Show me," I insisted.

"Do I have to?"

"Yes."

She pointed the gun at the wall, closed her eyes and pulled the trigger with a click. Her tiny hand had trouble reaching around the handle even though this gun had been designed for women. She proved she could fire it once, although she might have had trouble firing it again in rapid succession.

"What did you do after you fired the gun?"

"I ran home and threw it in the ditch."

"Where?"

"Between here and there." She stared wistfully at my blank computer screen. "I don't think my mom's gonna make me go to school today. Would you mind if I played with Digital Schoolhouse or got on the Internet for a while?"

"Not now," I said. "I have to go to work. Tell your mother I'll call her this afternoon."

"You can't. She disconnected the phone. She said too many boys were calling."

"Then tell her I'll stop by after work. You stay home all day with your mother and you keep the door locked. All right?"

"All right."

I walked her to the door and watched until her mother opened the door and let her into the trailer. When I crossed the courtyard again I spotted Sonia's butt on the bricks. I picked it up, took it inside and dropped it in the trash.

5

On my way downtown
I took a detour to the District Attorney's office to visit my old friend and occasional adversary, Deputy DA Anthony Saia. He still had his creased, rumpled Sunday-morning-in-bed look, although his hair had turned Saturday-night slick. He had the kind of hair that reacted to every change in humidity and wind—before he started spraying it. He hadn't sprayed his desk, however, and that was still a mess. Having a computer hadn't prevented him from accumulating a pile of papers that was six inches thick and in constant motion. If he sneezed, a document would fall off. His walls were cluttered with diplomas and pho-

tos of himself at various stages of his legal career. Rowing a boat at Yale, smiling with President Clinton when the Pres came to town, eating Chinese with Raymond Ko at the Ko Palace. But the most prominent spot on the wall was occupied by a mirror tipped so that Saia could see into it without getting up from his desk.

"Hey, Neil," he said. "How's it going?"

"Pretty good. New hairdo?" I asked.

He ran his hand over his helmet-smooth head. "Oh, yeah. I haven't seen you for a while, have I?"

"Nope." There was only one reason I could think of for Anthony Saia to change his look. "New woman?"

He grinned. "That, too."

"Anybody I know?"

"Her name is Jennifer Spaulding. She's a clerk for Judge Raymond Stone."

"A law clerk?"

"Yeah. She works out with a personal trainer. Great abs."

"I see a few more gray ones, Anthony." It was a lie, but a deputy DA ought to know a lie when he hears one.

"Where?" he said, turning toward the mirror.

"Just kidding."

"Ha, ha. So what's new with you?"

"I quit smoking." Saia was a guy who worked out

with a pack of cigarettes, a hard-core nonfiltered Camel addict who'd been known to keep two cigarettes burning at once. I checked his desk and saw no overflowing ashtrays or smoking butts. "You too?" Was that a side effect of being involved with a law clerk?

"Naah. They turned this into a nonsmoking office, so now I have to go outside. Bad thing to do to a public servant. It could be enough to send me into private practice." That was one change I didn't think Saia would ever make; this man was born to prosecute. "How's your life going?"

"Good. I bought a house."

"Where?"

"In the North Valley."

"Yeah?" He rubbed his fingers together in the universal gesture of money and greed. The North Valley is one of Albuquerque's more affluent neighborhoods, but not the street that I live on.

"Not that part of the Valley," I said.

"Where is it?"

"On Mirador east of Fourth."

"There was a shooting in that neighborhood recently, a kid named Juan Padilla."

"So I hear."

"Is this the visit of a concerned citizen?" He knew I didn't stop by just to shoot the shit.

"Not exactly."

"Anything you want to tell me about Juan Padilla's death? You know something I don't?"

"What do you know?"

"We have a witness who ID'd the shooter as Ron Cade, a member of a Heights gang." That was no revelation; it had been all over the news.

"Your witness is reliable?"

"He gave the police a very accurate description of the shooter."

If he was thinking the same thing I was—that the witness's description might be too accurate—he gave no indication. "The sketch was very close to Ron Cade's photo," I said.

"There was a strong resemblance. It was either Cade or his evil twin," Saia agreed. "The police artist does good work."

"What's your witness's name?"

"I'd rather not give it out until I have to. He's a juvenile. There's always the danger of gang retaliation."

"Is he a gang member?" That would make any witness less credible in my book.

"No."

"The witness didn't see anybody but Cade?"

"No."

"And you believe Ron Cade acted alone?" In my experience teenagers joined gangs because they didn't like to act alone.

"That's what the witness said."

"That'll make it easier for you guys. Only one perp to track down."

"Unless Padilla's gang gets to him first. Their system of justice is swift and effective. Ours?" He threw up his hands.

"Are you ever tempted just to stay out of the way and let them duke it out?"

"It would save the taxpayers some money," Saia said. "A Four O shoots Ron Cade in retaliation for Juan Padilla's death, which was probably in retaliation for some other gang member's death. Then a Heights Highlifer has to kill a Four O in retaliation for Ron Cade. Once the killers are dead we turn them into heroes. That's the American way. Trouble is, a gangbanger's idea of justice can be to drive down the street shooting at anyone wearing the wrong color. We're not always right either, but we do put more effort into our justice than they put into theirs."

"This state has a lingering admiration for Billy the Kid."

"Hero worship is more like it. If you ask me, he was New Mexico's original gangbanger. This is a great country, isn't it? We give children TV and teenagers automatic weapons. Prison is our only deterrent, but that's no threat—their friends and family are already there. Civilization is a thin veneer.

All it takes is one tear in the social fabric and we revert to tribal warfare. Look at Bosnia, look at Africa, look at L.A. We're a backwater compared to them. At least our gang members are still loyal to each other. In L.A. the gangs have gotten so big they're fighting for power on the inside and shooting their own homeboys. The killing goes on and on, but the police have to step in somewhere or the citizens think the streets aren't safe for them. Too many ricocheting bullets."

"I hear the murder weapon was a thirty-eight."

"Oh, yeah? Where'd you hear that?" He'd picked up a rubber band and begun fiddling with it.

I ignored his question and continued with one of mine. "Don't you think it unusual for a gang slaying to involve a revolver?"

He shrugged. "Gang members have access to all kinds of guns."

"I also heard that Juan was killed with one round."

"So?" He stretched the rubber band taut between his fingers.

"I guess that means the perp was a good shot."

"Or got lucky."

"Did Juan fire, too?"

"No. He didn't even get a round off. I hope you're not considering representing Ron Cade, Neil. His parents have the bucks to pay you well, but he's a monster, a superpredator. I almost got him last year on breaking and entering, but he slipped away. If you are going to represent him and you're thinking self-defense, you can forget it."

"If prison is no threat, why do you care about locking up Ron Cade?"

"It would keep him off the streets, and I wouldn't have to look at his face again for a while. Stay away from that guy, Neil. Trust me, you wouldn't want to end up on his bad side."

"You get on a lot of people's bad sides, don't you?" Only last week a gang member attacked a prosecutor in court after receiving a murder conviction. It didn't help the guy's case any when sentencing rolled around.

"I look at those punks day after day in the courtroom, but they don't scare me," Saia said. "I go home and I sleep very well, thank you. So are you planning on representing Ron Cade?"

"No."

"Good." He snapped his fingers and the rubber band sprung loose across his desk. "We came that close to nabbing him yesterday," he told me. "That close." He placed his thumb and index finger a hair's width apart. "He passed a unmarked highway patrolman on I–40 doing ninety miles an hour. The patrolman lost him at Tijeras."

It's pretty hard to lose anybody in Tijeras, which

is just a dot on the Interstate map. "How did that happen?"

"The patrolman spun out on the exit ramp."

"Didn't he call for backup?"

"Yeah, but by the time the backup got there Cade had disappeared into the East Mountains." The East Mountains, a forested area on the backside of the Sandias, is a place where bodies—alive or dead— often disappear.

"He keeps showing his face in public taunting us," Saia continued. "Or the Four O's. This could be one area where our interests coincide. Here's a picture taken on his last trip to court." He dove into the pile on his desk and pulled out a photo. "Nice guy, huh?"

The suspect, who was being led from the courtroom with his hands in cuffs and his legs in restraints, was snarling like he was getting ready to spit at the camera, his mouth being the only weapon he could still use. "What do you want to do? Wipe the sneer off his face?"

"Something like that," Saia said. "I got a witness, I got an impulsive and remorseless suspect, I got a motive. You're not going to complicate a simple gangbang homicide for me, are you?"

"I hope not."

He looked at his watch. "Anything else, Neil? I've got a meeting coming up."

"A meeting or a cigarette?"

"Both." He laughed. "Smoke now, meet later."

"I'm done."

He looked in the mirror, touched his hair to make sure every strand was slicked in place, stood up and shook my hand. "Whatever you're considering, it's always a pleasure for me to work with you."

"Thanks, Anthony," I said. But this was one time when the pleasure would likely be all his.

After I left his office I went to Walgreen's and bought a pack of Nicorette gum. Next I stopped at Java Joe's and got a coffee to go—black and shiny as an oil slick, no milk, no sugar, no Coffee-mate powder floating on top. I took the coffee and gum to my office, waved to Anna who was talking on the phone, picked up the mail, went into my office and closed the door. There was nothing in the mail that couldn't wait, so I sipped at my coffee, unwrapped the stick of gum, popped it in my mouth, picked up a pen and began drawing diamonds down the side of a yellow legal pad.

What I'd deduced from my meeting with Anthony Saia was that the weapon could have been a thirty-eight and that only one bullet had been fired. Saia had neither admitted nor denied those facts, but I knew his reactions well enough to know when I'd stumbled on the truth. Most gangbangers got off a few rounds, if only for the pleasure of doing it. Maybe there had been only one shot because a small hand had been holding the gun. I didn't know whether Cheyanne was guilty, but she knew too much to be completely innocent. Saia had made it clear that the person he wanted to prosecute was Ron Cade, but as far as I knew all he had working for him was a witness. Ron Cade might have had a motive for the shooting, but there was no weapon yet. As for the witness, who knew what his motives were?

I filled in the blanks in the first diamond and moved on down the page. I had agreed to represent a thirteen-year-old girl who might or might not be guilty of murder, who might or might not know something that would put Ron Cade away. The one question I had to keep asking myself was, What was in her best interest?

After work I stopped at the double-wide to make sure my client was staying home. A truck with ladders attached to the roof was parked in front of the trailer on the spot where some people might have planted a lawn. I knocked at the screen door, which had a metal frame and a deadbolt lock. That was good. A guy with a chain tattooed on his forearm answered my knock—that wasn't so good. He wore a white short-sleeved shirt. His name, Leo, was embroidered on the pocket on one side of his chest and the name of the company he worked for, Coss Plumbing, was embroidered on the other. That and the ladder made him an air-conditioning repairman, one of those jobs that takes men in and out of women's houses. His tight shirt showed the beginnings of a belly, but his arms were muscular and hard. He had short dark hair and a cautious smile. I could hear a TV playing somewhere inside the trailer and a baby crying.

"I'm Neil Hamel," I said. "I live down the street."

"Leo Ortega. Danny's father."

"Is Sonia here?"

"She went to work."

"How about Cheyanne?"

"She's here. Come on in."

"I'd rather talk to her outside, if you don't mind."

"Sonia doesn't want her to leave the house."

"It's okay. I'm her lawyer."

"Cheyanne!" he yelled.

She came to the door with Miranda wailing in her arms. "Could you turn the crying off, please?" I asked.

"Okay." She turned the key.

I walked her away from the trailer to the far side of Leo Ortega's truck. "Have you been staying home?" I asked her.

"Are you kidding me?" She poked the ground

with the toe of her running shoe. "My mom don't let me go nowhere. After she went to work today, Leo showed up, and he's even worse than she is. He won't give me no air."

"It's for your own good," I said. And where had I heard that before? From an adult who had pissed me off when I was her age. Nothing like hanging around a teenager to make you realize that what goes around comes around—and sooner than you think.

"He's not my father," Cheyanne said.

"I know. Does he come here often?"

"Sometimes."

"To see Danny?"

"That's what he says. But then he gets on *la teta . . .*"

The tit, aka the bottle.

". . . and he and my mom . . . you know."

I knew, but I didn't recommend it. There's a reason why people who split up stay that way. Drifting in and out of a relationship is too much time, trouble and pain. "Could your mother bring you to my office before she goes to work tomorrow, say around three-thirty? I'll bring you home."

"Okay," she said.

For dinner the Kid got a bag of stuffed *sopaipillas* with green chile from Casa de Benavidez. You can count on Casa de Benavidez chile to make you weep.

"Did you know that they have *sopaipillas* in Argentina?" he asked me.

"Every country has something with dough that gets stuffed, don't they?"

"Yeah, but they call them different things in different places. Bariloche in Argentina and here are the only places I know where they call them *sopaipillas*. I didn't think I would see that word when I came here."

Like fog, colloquial Spanish has a way of settling into mountain villages. There are places in northern New Mexico where they still speak a form of Castilian.

Before opening the bag, getting the plates and starting dinner, I told him I'd been to see Anthony Saia.

"Who's that?"

"The deputy DA. Remember? I've worked with him before."

"Oh, yeah."

Then I told him I was representing Cheyanne and that she wanted to plead guilty to the murder of Juan Padilla.

The Kid didn't buy it. "You believe that little girl killed somebody?"

I had to admit that I didn't know. "Saia is willing to accept the witness's version of events that Ron

Cade killed Juan Padilla and that he acted alone."

"That's good for the girl, no?"

"Yes and no. If she were an adult it would be one thing, but I have a hard time telling a thirteen-year-old who confesses to murder to forget about it and walk away."

"Maybe the witness is telling the truth."

"It's not the whole truth. Cheyanne knows too much about the crime."

"Do you know who the witness is?"

"No. Saia wouldn't tell me."

The Kid took a sip of his Tecate. "You want me to see what I can find out?"

"How?"

"Talk to the boys who come into the shop."

"Okay." Be discreet, I might have added, but asking the Kid to be careful with words was like asking anybody else to be careful with hundred-dollar bills. "Cheyanne knows more about the crime than Saia would reveal," I said. "Either she was there or she's talked to someone who was."

"Ron Cade?"

"If that's who she was with at the ditch, the opportunity existed to exchange information."

"What happens if she confesses?"

"If Saia believes her, she'll be sent to the Detention Home until sentencing and then to the Girls' School for two years."

"It could be better for her than being on the street, no?"

"In some ways the D Home and the Girls' School are just an extension of the street. Gangs can operate inside almost as well as they do outside."

"What happens to this Ron Cade if Cheyanne says she did it?"

"Hard to say. There doesn't seem to be much evidence. There's Cheyanne's story and the witness's story and Ron Cade's story—whatever that is. Cade could be charged with being an accessory or he could walk."

That was all there was to say at the moment, so we opened the bag. The chile was as hot as I'd hoped. Green chile can be like going to see *Bambi* or *Gone with the Wind*. It'll bring on the tears you can't always summon yourself.

Before we went to bed I turned on the burglar alarm and checked the back patio. A cat I had never seen before was nibbling on my catnip. It was gray and scrawny and its ribs were visible under the mangy fur. It spotted my shape through the glass door, stared for a minute with fierce eyes and ran away.

6

The following afternoon
Cheyanne and Sonia showed up in my office wearing their respective uniforms, an extra large t-shirt featuring a bull for Cheyanne, a short skirt and green Sandia Indian Bingo t-shirt for Sonia. I happened to be standing at my window looking out through the burglar bars when they arrived. Sonia parked her Toyota beside the curb and slammed the door shut. They came up the walkway showing me the faces they wore when they weren't talking to their lawyer. Cheyanne's expression was surly. Sonia's was pissed. She took one last drag on her cigarette and flipped it under the thistle that bloomed

with poisonous purple vigor beside the sidewalk.

Anna asked if they wanted something to drink. Sonia had a coffee with sugar. Cheyanne had a Coke. They came into my office and sat down on the other side of the desk.

Sonia tried to suppress a yawn. "Long night," she said.

"I saw Deputy DA Anthony Saia yesterday," I began. "He specializes in gang violence, and Juan Padilla's shooting is his case."

"Did you tell him I did it?" Cheyanne had that wide-eyed look kids who've been arrested get in front of the camera. They know they've done something bad, but they're excited by all the attention. When the cameras have departed and they're alone in their cells, these same kids are capable of killing themselves.

"No," I said. The buzz went out of Cheyanne and she slumped in her chair.

"Why not?" Sonia asked.

"Saia's witness ID'd Ron Cade as the shooter and the witness said Cade acted alone. The DA's office is willing to go with that."

"Did they find the gun?" Sonia asked.

"I don't think so."

Sonia's fingers did a tap dance along the edge of my desk. "Do you know this guy Ron Cade?" she asked her daughter.

Cheyanne squirmed. "I've talked to him is all. I don't really know him."

"Was he there that night?"

"No," Cheyanne mumbled.

"You sure?"

"I told you he wasn't."

"Is this guy trying to get you to confess for him?" Sonia asked. She'd arrived at the same thought I had, although with less information.

"It's not like that. I did it," Cheyanne cried. "What do I have to do to make you believe me?" The anguish in her voice was real. She wasn't emoting for an imaginary camera now.

One reason nobody wanted to believe her was that she had the face of a child and the hair of an angel. She was twisting one of her baby curls around and around on her finger. Her language, however, came up out of the street. "Fucking DA, fucking lawyers, fucking everybody," she swore.

"Watch your mouth!" Sonia warned.

It was my job to remain cool and collected. "Saia would rather prosecute a seventeen-year-old than a thirteen-year-old," I said.

"I only get two years, right?" Cheyanne asked.

"Right."

"I'll do it. Being in the Girls' School is better than being locked up with you and Leo." She turned toward her mother.

"You're a little monster," Sonia snapped. "You know that."

"Look," I said. "The best thing to do right now is wait and see what the police investigation turns up. I can't make Saia put Cheyanne in detention. But you've got to stay home until this is resolved. No going to school. No hanging out with your friends."

"That's worse than being in prison," Cheyanne complained.

"She'll do it," said Sonia.

Sonia had to get to her job at the bingo parlor. I had work to do, so Cheyanne hung out in the reception room waiting for me and talking hair with Anna. When I came out of my office, her bangs were slick and wide and sticking straight up.

"The teachers call this the flyswatter," Cheyanne said.

"Cool," said Anna. "How do kids get those really bright colors in their hair?"

"They use Jell-O. It makes your hair sticky so you can twist it around."

"Jell-O heads." Anna laughed.

That was one use for it. "You ready to roll?" I asked Cheyanne.

"Okay with me," she said.

I led her out back to where the Nissan was

parked. Cheyanne sniffed when she sat down in the passenger seat. "Smells like my mom's," she said. "Looks like my mom's, too."

"How's that?"

"Like a purse on wheels."

The Nissan was on the messy side, I'll admit it. "I'm cleaning it this weekend."

"That's what my mom always says."

I wasn't in the mood to drive past the D Home on Second, so I took us home by way of Fourth Street. A drive can be a good place to have a heart-to-heart. Sometimes truths will come out in motion that don't when you're sitting still. This wasn't a very long drive, so I started as soon as we pulled out of the parking lot.

"You know, Cheyanne," I began, "a murderer who gets away with it once is liable to do it again. If Saia should accept your plea and you're not guilty, you could be allowing a killer to go free. Is that what you want?"

"Nobody's going free," she answered with such conviction that if she'd been older she'd have followed her statement with "trust me."

"You should tell your mother about you and Ron Cade beside the ditch."

"I can't," she said.

We lapsed into silence. Thirteen-year-olds are not the world's best conversationalists and negotiating Fourth Street required a certain amount of finesse, so we continued in silence. Cheyanne stared out the window while we passed Garcia's Family Restaurant, Silverado, the Montano intersection where the traffic was backed up for blocks waiting to turn left and cross the river, Dan's Boots and Saddles and Los Chamisos, where a ten-acre alfalfa field had been turned into a gated luxury home community. In front of Casa Home Repair a kid with dazzling red hair and a ring through his nose waited to cross the street.

"Jell-O head?" I asked my companion.

"Yeah."

"What flavor?"

"Raspberry," she replied.

I passed Diamond Shamrock and turned the corner onto Mirador. We saw Danny biking down the road with a pole in one hand.

Cheyanne rolled down her window. "Hey, bro," she yelled.

I pulled over beside Danny and saw that his pole was dangling a large plastic worm. "Going fishing?" I asked.

He nodded.

"You dork," Cheyanne said. "There aren't any fish in the ditch."

"You don't know that," said Danny.

"Is your dad picking you up?" Cheyanne asked.

"Yeah."

"Good," she said. "Than I can stay home alone."

Which could mean going out alone. "No way," I said. "You can stay at my house till your mother gets home from work."

"Do I have to?"

"Yes, you have to."

Danny waved and headed toward the ditch.

"Can we go to the trailer first?" Cheyanne asked. "There's something I want to show you."

"Okay."

Leo hadn't arrived yet, and there were no vehicles parked in front of the double-wide. I told Cheyanne to leave a note for her mother telling her she'd be at my place. While Cheyanne went inside, I looked at the bare yard thinking that scraping could be easier than watering, weeding, spraying and cutting.

Cheyanne came back trailing Tabatoe behind her and holding something in her hand. She sat down beside me, pulled the car door shut and handed over a plastic Ziploc bag containing a spent bullet. The bullet was about a half-inch long, flat and narrow at one end and mushroomed at the other. There was some debris on the wide end—blood, dirt or flesh.

Cheyanne flipped her hair over her shoulder and looked me in the eye. "Do you believe me now?" she asked.

"Where'd you get it?"

"It hit the wall after it went through Juan and I picked it up off the ground. If you show that to the DA, will he believe me?"

"He might."

"Good," she said.

I called the Kid when we got to my house and told him to bring home a few more tacos for dinner. Cheyanne wanted to get on Teen Chat and I said go ahead. It couldn't be any worse than the things she'd already experienced. When I told her to turn the computer off and come to dinner she groaned, "Now?"

"Now," I said.

Cheyanne complained that the tacos were too hot and drank a lot of water, but she ate every bite. Tabatoe's face appeared at the glass door and Cheyanne asked me if she could come in, but I told her I ran a no-cat household. After dinner we watched TV. Cheyanne fell asleep on the sofa. I took that opportunity to show the Kid the bullet. "She says it's the bullet that killed Juan Padilla."

"Do you believe her?" he asked.

"I don't know."

"What are you going to do with it?"

"Talk to Sonia."

The Kid went to bed, but I sat up, watched TV and waited for Sonia. Around midnight the doorbell rang.

"My daughter's here?" Sonia asked.

"Yeah."

We went into the kitchen and I turned on the light. "There's something I need to show you," I said, holding up the plastic bag with the spent bullet inside.

"Where'd that come from?"

"Your daughter."

Sonia pulled a cigarette out of her purse but stopped herself and put it back. "Can they prove it was the bullet that killed Juan Padilla if they don't find the gun?"

"With DNA testing they probably can."

"Son of a bitch," she said. "Are you going to turn it over to that DA? What's his name?"

"Saia. What do you want me to do?"

"What does Cheyanne want to do?"

"Turn it over."

"Do it," she said.

Cheyanne was sleeping peacefully as a baby, but she swore and kicked when Sonia woke her up. As I walked them back through the living room I noticed that the computer was still on and the screen saver was flitting across the screen. After the Morans left I turned the computer off and walked around the house looking for a good place to stash the bullet. The safest place I could think of was the drawer in the nightstand, beside my thirty-eight, next to my pillow. I got into bed and curled up behind the Kid, who was already asleep. Around four the temperature dropped and I woke up and covered us with a sheet. I'd been dreaming that there was a boardwalk behind my house and an animal lived under it that was a combination rattlesnake and cat. I could see its eyes smiling up at me through the spaces between the boards. The animal had thick orange and white fur and its long tail had rattles at the tip. The fur was so silky I wanted to reach down and pet it, but then it snarled and rattled its tail.

7

When I woke up again
the Kid had left for work and the bullet and gun were
still in the drawer. On my way downtown I drove
past the D Home. A bunch of gangsters in baggy
clothes were standing outside waiting for their probation officers. In order to get in and out of this place
you had to run a gangbanger gauntlet. I called Saia
as soon as I got to my office and made an appoint-
ment to see him that afternoon. I was holding up the
plastic bag and looking at the bullet when Anna
walked into my office.

"Where'd that come from?" she asked.

"Cheyanne. She says she picked it up off the

ground after it went through Juan Padilla and rico-
cheted off a wall."

"You really think that little girl shot somebody?"

"Maybe it wasn't a cold-blooded, calculated
shooting, but frightened, in self-defense? Who
wouldn't be capable under those circumstances?"

"If you have a gun in your hand."

"A lot of things are possible when you have a
loaded gun in your hand."

"She seems so innocent."

"Sometimes. Sometimes she doesn't seem innocent at all."

"Where'd she get the gun? Steal it from her
mother?"

That was one road I hadn't traveled down yet.
"Maybe."

"Gangs use semiautomatics, don't they?"

"Usually." One advantage to semiautomatics is
that you can get so many rounds off so fast that accu-
racy hardly matters. You can spray your opponent
into oblivion. The disadvantage is that semiautomatics can leave an all-too-easy-to-trace casing on the
ground. But when it comes to shootings, gang members don't often worry about evidence and what
comes after. Their motto seems to be shoot now,
think later.

"What are you going to do?" Anna asked.

"Turn it over to Anthony Saia," I said.

* * *

When I got to Saia's office that afternoon every hair was slicked in place. His eyes were bright with a prosecutor's zeal, but that was a fire I was about to put out. "What's up?" he asked.

"I have the bullet that killed Juan Padilla." I handed over the plastic bag.

"How'd you get this?"

"From my client, a thirteen-year-old girl named Cheyanne Moran."

"How'd she get it?"

"She picked it up off the ground after it went through the victim."

"You're going to tell me she was a witness, right?"

"Wrong. I'm telling you she wants to plead guilty to manslaughter in the case of Juan Padilla."

That took the light from his eyes and the spray from his hair. His clothes already looked like they'd been through the wringer. "You're giving me a thirteen-year-old shooter?"

"I am."

"What the hell can I do to a thirteen-year-old girl?" It was a rhetorical question; he knew the answer better than I.

"Put her in the Girls' School for two years."

"She comes from a broken home? Right? Absent

father? Mother works all the time or takes drugs? Fatherless, godless, jobless and hopeless."

"Something like that."

"The Girls' School will seem like summer camp."

"That's a possibility."

"I could go for consecutive two-year terms and hold her over until she is twenty-one."

"You won't get away with it."

"Let's say she was an accessory. Cade's her boyfriend and she's covering for him. She's crazy about the guy and she wants to save his neck. I can put him away for life, but she'll only get two years. So she pleads guilty for him."

It was one scenario.

"If she gives him up I'll deal," Saia said.

"What are you offering? A trip to Europe? A new car? A father? A new life?"

"I would if I could."

Avoiding the Girls' School didn't seem to be any bargaining chip with my client. "I'll run it by her, Anthony, but I don't think she'll go for it. She says she acted alone."

He leaned back in his chair. "I find that hard to believe."

He wasn't the only one.

"Where's the weapon?" he asked.

"She says she threw it in the ditch."

"Can she show us where?"

"I'll ask her."

"Don't ask her, tell her."

"When it comes to teenagers, nobody tells them nothing, don't you know that yet?"

"It won't be like that when I have a family."

"Don't count on it."

"I'll have the bullet analyzed to see if it was the one that killed Padilla."

"It's in your hands," I said.

He flipped a pencil up on its tip and began poking the point into the pile of papers on his desk. "There is one more thing. Cade's lawyer called and arranged to bring him in for questioning." He laughed. "Maybe I'll end up with two guilty pleas."

"Not likely," I said.

DNA analysis of the bullet would take time. Dredging the ditch could be done quickly, but more easily with Cheyanne's cooperation. The APD could have searched the ditch without her. They could have followed the Chapuzar Lateral from the crime scene to Mirador Road, but they wanted Cheyanne to go to the scene with them to show them how and where she had shot Juan Padilla and to pinpoint the spot where she'd dumped the gun.

I stopped by the trailer the following morning and found Cheyanne, Sonia and Leo sitting around

the table having a cup of coffee before they went to
bed or to work or stayed home all day and watched
the tube. Tabatoe was curled up in Cheyanne's lap.
On the wall an orange tiger paced across a black vel-
vet background. I looked out through the kitchen
window and saw pigeons lined up like targets on the
telephone line. I told Cheyanne that I'd given the
bullet to Saia.

"Will he believe me now?" she asked. Her eyes
were wide.

I glanced at Leo. I wasn't sure this case should be
discussed in front of anyone but Sonia and
Cheyanne. "It's all right," Sonia said. "Leo's in on
what's happening."

"Is it all right with you?" I asked Cheyanne.

She studied her chipped fingernails. "I guess."

"Is that a yes or a no?"

"It's an all right," she said.

I took that as a sign to continue. "If you were with
Ron Cade and he shot Padilla, you could be charged
with being an accessory. Saia will cut a deal if you tell
him Ron Cade was the shooter."

Leo put his elbows on the table. He was wearing
an undershirt and I could see the black curly hair on
his chest, the chain on his right forearm and the Virgin of Guadalupe tattooed on his left bicep. "What
kind of deal are they willing to cut?" he asked.

"Very little or no time at all in the Girls' School,

I'd say. Saia has a vendetta against Cade, plus Cade is too old to be treated as a juvenile. Saia would prefer to prosecute him."

Cheyanne stared at the crumbs on the Formica table and said nothing.

"Listen up," Leo ordered.

She raised her head and flipped her hair over her shoulder. Tabatoe leapt off her lap. "Ron Cade didn't do it, I did. Got it?"

"Don't get smart with me," Leo snapped.

"You're not my father."

Sonia's cigarette was burning in the ashtray and the smoke was rising like a warning signal from a fire. "Knock it off, you two," she said.

Leo shut his mouth, but he tightened his grip on his coffee mug until the virgin on his muscle shivered. Had he gotten those muscles from lifting the ladder? I wondered. From emptying the water out of evaporative coolers? Or was it from pumping iron?

"Do either of you own a thirty-eight?" I asked Sonia and Leo.

"I didn't get it from them," Cheyanne said.

"Who did you get it from?"

"I can't tell you."

"I don't keep guns anymore," said Leo.

"I never kept guns," said Sonia. "Coffee?" she asked me.

"No thanks. Saia is threatening to ask for consecutive two-year terms and to hold you over until you are twenty-one, Cheyanne. It will go better for you if you cooperate."

"I already said I did it. What else do they want?"

"Saia wants you to show the APD where you threw the weapon."

"In the ditch, I said."

"They want to know where in the ditch."

"Do I have to?" She wrapped a curl around her finger and tugged at her hair.

"DNA testing may prove that bullet killed Juan. It won't prove that you're the one who fired it. The gun could help if your prints are on it."

"But if we go to the ditch everybody will see me," she moaned.

"Do it," barked Leo.

"All right, all right."

8

When the time came to
search the ditch the police swarmed all over the Chapuzar Lateral and the neighboring fields like mosqui-
toes after a hard rain. They'd searched the area before,
but their search hadn't been nearly as thorough or
precise. A ditch rider made the job easier by stopping
the flow further north and letting the relevant part of
the ditch network drain out. Instead of brown muddy
water in the Chapuzar Lateral there was thick, brown
mud. It resembled the ruts that pass for rivers in this
part of the country.

Cheyanne prepared for the search by pumping
up the volume of her hair and putting on her largest

t-shirt. Sonia took the afternoon off from work. The Morans, the investigating officers and I began at the strip mall. There were two officers: a tall, rangy guy with intense blue eyes named Jim Donaldson and Sandra Jessup, a plump woman with fine brown hair. She had blue eyes, too, but hers had a twinkle in them. His had long distance.

Cheyanne pointed out where Juan had fallen, approximately where she had stood when she shot him, and the place where she had found the bullet. She insisted that the gun had gone off accidentally but wouldn't say where she got it or who else was there. She said she'd been talking to Juan before the shooting happened, but she wouldn't say what they'd been talking about.

After we'd examined the crime scene we walked down Ladera toward the ditch, turning onto the access road at the corner where people dump their mattress springs and worn-out refrigerators. Donaldson and Jessup walked with Cheyanne, Sonia and me. A third officer named Tony Mares followed inside the ditch, which had to be like walking through a bled dry vein. The ground was wet, and it was slow going for him as the mud sucked at his boots. Rotting apples clustered at the first culvert we came to. They were covered with buzzing flies that were turning iridescent in the sun. I smelled the apples long before I saw them. It was the smell of a changing season. The air was already showing some of the coolness of fall, when the sun no longer pounds you into the pavement.

Cheyanne was way nervous. Her eyes darted from the ditch to the fields to the houses and back again. Her hands tugged at the hem of her t-shirt. She walked quickly. The detectives let her go at her own pace. Maybe they thought she knew where she was headed, but I wasn't so sure. Sonia followed behind us puffing on a cigarette. After we passed the culvert and crossed the first street, Detective Donaldson gave Detective Jessup a sideways glance. I knew what they were thinking. Wouldn't Cheyanne have tossed the gun as soon as she got to the ditch? Why wait?

Detective Mares wrestled with the mud and fell behind. The drained ditch resembled an archaeological dig loaded with the relics of late-twentieth-century Rio Grande valley civilization—beer cans, the tiny liquor bottles known as miniatures, running shoes, sandals, a cowboy boot, the pale white skeleton of a long-dead bird, a sprinkling of condoms, a doll, a rifle, a rusty semiautomatic pistol. Every time Mares came across something of interest he stopped and examined it. He lifted the semiautomatic carefully and dropped it in an evidence bag.

We passed behind the Kid's shop with the flying red horse sign, the Renewal Spa and Beauty Salon, the Armijo wood yard, La Cienega gated community and the Texas Trailer Ranch and came to a place where the weeds on the bank were taller than Cheyanne. Beside us was an empty field. It was the same place I'd found her struggling with Ron Cade. What had been dark and shadowy at night was dry and empty during the day. Cheyanne stopped here and stared at the field, trembling like a flower in the wind.

"Is this the place?" Detective Jessup asked.

Cheyanne shook her head and kept on walking. We went on like this until we were only one block away from Mirador. By now school had let out. The police kept everybody away from the ditch, but from this location we could see the kids walking home from school. A couple of guys stopped, looked at us, then shuffled on down the road. They wore long black t's and wide pants, the shape that said gang. Danny rode by on his bike. Patricia leaned against a tree and watched us until a cop made her move on.

Cheyanne jumped off the ditch bank into a field where there was a barrier of Siberian elms between her and Mirador Road. "This is the place. This is where I threw it," she said.

Detective Mares, who had caught up to us, said, "I thought you said you threw it in the ditch."

Cheyanne shook her head. "I was wrong," she whispered. "It went in here. Can I go home now?"

But the APD wasn't ready to let her go. The police made her cover the field with them, inch by inch, but too much time had gone by, too many animals and people had moved through here. If the gun had ever been in this field, it was long gone.

The police continued their search, but after an hour they let Cheyanne, Sonia and I go. I walked them as far as my courtyard, where Patricia stood waiting.

"Everybody could see you, Cheyanne," she said.

"I know," Cheyanne moaned.

"What did you tell them?"

"Cheyanne shouldn't be discussing this case with anybody, and that includes you," I said to Patricia.

"But I'm her friend." Patricia poked the ground with her foot and kicked up some dust.

"You can talk about it when it's settled," I said.

"Okay," mumbled Cheyanne. She was about as down as a thirteen-year-old can get, which is way down.

Patricia tried to cheer her up. "That cop that was talking to me? Do you know his name?" she asked.

"No," said Cheyanne.

"He's fine."

"He's a cop."

"I'll see you later," Patricia said. "I gotta catch the bus and go home." She headed west toward Fourth Street.

After she left Sonia asked me the question that had been on her mind. "Are they going to arrest Cheyanne now?"

"Without the gun? I doubt it," I said. I'd ended up in the awkward position of trying to get a client into jail. "I don't think they'll do anything before they talk to Ron Cade and get the DNA back on the bullet."

"What's gonna happen to her, then? Everyone will know she's been talking to the police now."

"The timing of the search was not good," I agreed.

"She's like a piece of cheese for a rat, and there are plenty of rats in this town."

"Keep an eye on her. Keep her at home," I advised. "And you, you listen to your mother, Cheyanne."

"Okay," she mumbled.

Cheyanne and Sonia headed home. I could see Leo's truck in the yard and I watched him open the door and let them in.

It was the night the garbage goes out, and after dinner I went around the house emptying wastepaper baskets into a black plastic bag.

"You want me to do that?" the Kid asked when I took the bag outside to load it into the garbage can, but he was buried in the sofa with a Tecate in his hand, so I said I'd do it myself.

I dumped the bag in the pail, closed the lid and lugged the garbage down the driveway, setting off my neighbor's motion detector light, which illuminated Danny standing at the end of the driveway holding the handlebars of his bike. The light cast a long shadow behind him and turned his tires into monster truck wheels.

"Can I help you?" he asked.

Helping seemed more important to him than it had to the Kid, so I let him.

Danny leaned his bike against the fence and walked toward me. The pail was about as tall as he was, but he took the handle and held up his end while we carried it down the driveway and parked it beside the road. Under the street lamp I could see that he was wearing his hair slicked up and back in a modified DA.

"New hairdo?" I asked him.

"Kinda."

"What do you call it?"

"The greaseball," he said.

"How do you get it to stay back like that?"

"Grease." He sat on the seat of his bike and put one foot on the ground for balance. The raised letters on his Goosebumps t-shirt shimmered beneath the street lamp.

"What are Goosebumps anyway?" I asked him.

"Books for kids."

"What do you like about them?"

"They're scary."

I thought real life was scary enough, but Goosebumps were a scare, maybe, he felt he could control. "Which one is your favorite?"

"*The Beast from the East.*" He fingered the tassel that hung from his handlebars. "Do you think my sister killed Juan Padilla?" he asked.

"She says she did."

"What do you think?"

It's hard to con a nine-year-old who has just helped you take out the trash, so I told him the truth as I saw it. "I don't know."

"But you would let her go to jail."

"It's not jail exactly, it's the D Home and then maybe the Girls' School."

"She'll be in there with kids who are in gangs and in trouble, right?"

"Right. If she goes. It was her decision to plead guilty, Danny. Hers and your mother's."

"My sister didn't kill anybody." His eyes were bright.

"How do you know?"

"I just know."

"If you're right, let's hope the police find the truth soon."

Having about as much faith in the police as an adult would, he got back on his bike and pedaled furiously down the street.

"Thanks for helping me with the garbage can," I called after him.

He looked back over his shoulder. "It's nothing," he yelled.

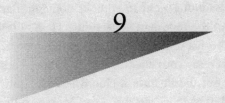

9

Saia and I met for lunch
downtown the following day at Conrad's in La Posada,
which was the first hotel in the Conrad Hilton chain.
Conrad had been a New Mexico boy. We took a window table, where you can watch the street people
stumble by pushing carts piled high with personal
junk. There's only a wall of glass between you and
them, and I'm always aware how thin a barrier it is,
the difference between being a street cat, for example,
or the well-fed Tabatoe.

Conrad's was nearly empty, although it used to
be packed at lunchtime when the food had a Spanish
flavor. But the chef had moved on, doing the Albu-

querque chef shuffle, and the food had degenerated into a hot and gloppy mess with a cheese meltdown on top.

"We should have gone somewhere else," I said.

But Saia dug right in without noticing that the quality of the food had gone south. He had crime-solving on his mind. "I read the police report," he began. "I'd say your client knew a lot about Padilla's murder but didn't have a clue where the gun was dumped. Detective Jessup says Moran suddenly picked a location when she saw that she was getting close to home and that all the other kids were out of school and watching her."

I had to give Jessup credit, because that was exactly the impression I'd had when Cheyanne jumped into the field. I'd thought she'd done it out of fear, but Saia seemed to be implying she'd done it for the attention. "The timing was bad, Anthony. She shouldn't have been out there when the other kids could see her with the police."

"Who knew how long the search was going to take?" Saia asked. "What you have is a witness, Neil, not a perp. I'm going to need more than you've given me to indict Cheyanne Moran."

"How about putting her in protective custody, then?"

"If she'll be a witness, I'll talk."

"She won't do that."

"No deal, then." Saia was eating soft, talking tough with a mouth full of beans and salsa.

"You're putting a thirteen-year-old girl in a dangerous position, Anthony. You leave her out on the street and she's bait."

"She always has the option of telling the truth. I'm sorry, Neil, but this perp story isn't cutting it for me. I'm under a lot of pressure to indict somebody for Padilla's murder, but I don't think your client's the one. I don't have the DNA back on the bullet yet and we need to interview some more people."

"It's your call," I said, but his call was leaving me with a low-level anxiety hum. Taos is famous for its hum. There are many people up there who claim they can hear it, but my own feeling about low-level hums is that they come from foreboding and conscience, not from place.

Saia finished his meal and looked down at his empty plate. "It seems that Ron Cade has an alibi," he said.

"How good?"

"I don't know. The boy who's supplying the alibi is out of town for a few days playing in a tennis tournament and we haven't been able to question him yet."

"A tennis tournament?"

"That's what Cade says."

"You'll let me know when you've checked it out?"

"Sure." Saia looked at his watch and said, "Gotta go."

He forgot to leave a tip, so I did it for him. I left more for him than I did for me, since he'd eaten his food.

Later that afternoon I called Sonia at Sandia Indian Bingo and passed on what Saia had said. Her response to my information was, "Shit."

"Keep Cheyanne at home," I advised.

When I got home after work Tabatoe was in my herb garden getting stoned on catnip and making me feel like the neighborhood drug dealer except that I wasn't getting paid for it. While Tabatoe purred and rolled in the dirt, the gray cat slinked around the corner switching its long tail and stepping lightly on silent paws. It snuck up behind Tabatoe at a leisurely pace, and when it was ready it pounced. Tabatoe let out a howl and raced down the driveway. I picked up a muddy running shoe and threw it at the gray cat. "Get out of here," I yelled. It took off, too, but when I looked out the window an hour later it was back again chowing down. A territorial battle had been fought in my herb garden, and the gray cat had won. My turf was now its turf, too.

I began to see it often, racing down my driveway, standing on the windowsill silhouetted against the glass while I was in the bathroom, pacing the courtyard's adobe wall, guarding my catnip and flicking its long gray tail. It seemed like an omen or a threat, always present, always edgy, always wanting something from me. The catnip didn't make it roll contentedly in the dirt. All the weed did was reduce its hunger pangs. When I complained to the Kid, he told me to feed it.

"If I feed it it will never go away," I said.

"At least it won't look so hungry," he said.

The following night I woke up when my neighbor's motion detector light flickered, went off, came back on again. My skylight was as bright as the moon and the light was turning the tree above it into a dancing shadow. The Kid groaned and pulled a pillow over his head. I lay still and listened. Except for my low-level anxiety hum, the night was very quiet; even the cicadas had ceased to scream. But the silence was filled with potential, and the potential I heard turned my spine to slush. I felt as if weights were pushing me deep in the bed.

There was a pounding on the street door. I jumped barefoot out of bed, ran across the bedroom, the living room and the courtyard. The gray cat stood on top of the adobe wall arching its back. "Get down," I yelled. I yanked open the door but found nothing on the stoop. All I saw was the streetlight turning weed shadows into stilettos. I looked up and down Mirador Road, but I didn't see a car, a bike, La Llorona or anything else in motion. The cat obeyed my command and jumped off the wall, and the motion detector light flickered off. I began to wonder if it wasn't the cat that had turned the light on in the first place and whether the pounding at the door had been a paranoid dream. I was about to go back to bed when I heard the squeal of a wounded animal on the far side of the courtyard. I stepped out the door and walked gingerly around the corner; my feet were still bare and the ground was full of prickers. I wondered whether I was going to find a victim of the gray cat or the victim of a human being. I found Cheyanne curled up in a ball between a piñon and the wall.

"Help me," she whimpered.

"Can you walk?"

"I think so."

I took her by the arms and lifted her up. She was smeared with blood. It came off on my hands when I touched her, although in this light it looked more like dark water than red blood. I took her hand and led her through the courtyard into the living room, leaving a trail of bloody footprints on the bricks and the floor.

"What happened? Were you shot?" I asked.

She shook her head. "Cut."

I took her into the bathroom and tried to stop the bleeding with a towel. Pieces of dried grass fell from her hair to the floor. She cried when I touched her, but I needed to find out where the blood was coming from if I was ever going to stop it. It seemed to be mostly face wounds, which bleed badly and could scar a girl for life. One towel soaked through and I grabbed another.

"Who did this to you?" I asked.

Her answer was a familiar refrain. "Don't make me tell you that. If I tell you they'll kill me."

"Where's your mother?"

"At the casino."

It wasn't as deep in the night as I'd thought if Sonia was still at work.

"And Leo?"

"He's at the trailer. Don't tell him. Please."

I'd taped some gauze to the worst cuts and got a better idea of what she looked like, which was worse than any of the nightmare looks teenagers create for themselves. Her hair was stained redder than raspberry Jell-O. Her cheeks were dirty, her eyes were swollen nearly shut.

The Kid appeared at the bathroom doorway. "I think we should take her to the hospital, chiquita," he said, which was all right with me. I'd already used up my limited knowledge of first aid. Cheyanne didn't protest, so we bundled her into the backseat of my car. When we passed the double-wide I saw that Leo's truck was there, that Sonia's car was not and that no lights were on. The Kid drove the Nissan through the canyons of downtown taking the corners like a race car driver. We had a good excuse for speeding if anyone stopped us, but nobody did.

We took her to the ER at Presbyterian. The doctor wore green scrubs and looked as if he'd seen too many wounds already that night. Lines were weary rivulets running down his face. After he examined and x-rayed Cheyanne he came out and talked to me.

"What's your relation to the victim?" he asked. "Mother?"

It was the first time I'd ever been accused of that. "Lawyer," I said.

"She'll be all right. No gunshot wounds, broken ribs, fractured skull, punctured lungs or other organs. I sewed up the gashes in her head, cleaned up the scrapes and bruises. She wasn't raped, you'll be glad to know."

"Good." The question of whether she was still a virgin went unasked and unanswered.

"Usually at this time of night it's gunshots: revolvers, rifles, semiautomatics, automatics. You name it, we get it. It's good training here for the next time the country goes to war. We don't see knife wounds so much anymore."

"That's what it was?"

"That's what it looks like to me. I called the police. They're on their way."

The cop who came over and took photos wanted to release Cheyanne into the custody of her mother, not her lawyer, but Sonia had already left the bingo parlor and could not be reached at home because she'd disconnected the phone. A police car was dispatched to pick her up.

The Kid, Cheyanne and I sat on a bench outside the ER and waited. Cheyanne, who was neatly bandaged and subdued, saw Sonia striding down the hallway before I did. "Uh-oh," she mumbled, staring into her lap. "Is she gonna be pissed."

Sonia did seem to be surrounded by a red aura of anger. When the Kid saw her expression he stood up, turned his back and walked down the hallway. "What in the hell have you done now?" Sonia yelled at her daughter.

"Nothin'," replied Cheyanne. "Somebody did somethin' to me. See?"

"You didn't get beat up inside the trailer, did you?"

"No."

"Wasn't Leo watching you?"

"He was watching television. I went to bed."

"How'd you get out?"

"Through my window."

"Why'd you do it? Why'd you get yourself into this mess?"

"I had to talk to somebody."

"Are you going to tell me who beat you?"

"No."

The Kid signaled me from the end of the hall-way. He had driving on his mind, so I interrupted the mother/daughter dialogue, which was nastier than any lawyer dialogue I'd ever been involved in. "Cheyanne needs to talk to the police tomorrow," I said. "Do you want to meet me at the police station or do you want me to take her?"

"Take her," Sonia said.

"Are they going to believe me now?" Cheyanne asked.

"It's possible," I replied.

Leaving the daughter to the mother's not-so-tender care, the Kid and I drove home through the empty streets. It was the middle of the night, we were on the road, it was a good place to have a heart-to-heart and we came about as close as we ever did.

"You think it's a good idea to leave the girl with a mother like that?" the Kid asked me.

"Maybe she's not the best mother, but she's the only mother Cheyanne has. Besides, this could be the last night they ever spend together."

"She's going into detention?"

"I hope so," I said. "Her life's not worth much on the street."

When we got home I picked the pieces of grass off the bathroom floor, put them in a Ziploc bag and stashed them in my desk drawer. Cheyanne had left bloody palm prints on the wall and the tile, but I was too tired to wash them off. The Kid and I went back to bed, although—for me anyway—not to sleep.

10

When I picked my client
up in the morning to take her to the police station she
was holding the baby doll Miranda in one arm and
her fat cat Tabatoe in the other. She kissed them good-
bye, put them down and patted Danny's hair. She
didn't have a single word or gesture for Leo and her
mother, who stood in the doorway and watched us go.

I'd hoped that Detective Sandra Jessup would be
on duty, and she was. I expected Jessup to be more
sympathetic to Cheyanne than Saia had been. Her
heart seemed less calcified.

She began by talking to Cheyanne gently and
looking at her bruises and her sewn-together face.

Jessup's baby-fine hair fell down as she bent over Cheyanne. Her hair and soft voice were a contrast to the severe suit she wore.

"Hurts, doesn't it?" she asked.

Cheyanne nodded.

"Your face looks bad right now, but that swelling will go away and soon you'll be yourself again."

"Really?"

"Trust me. You're a pretty girl and you have beautiful hair." Flattery was one approach I'd never considered.

"Thanks." Cheyanne tried to smile, but it hurt too much.

"Why would somebody do something like this to you?" Jessup asked.

"I don't know."

"Who did it?"

"I can't tell you that." Fear or loyalty or plain old stubbornness were stronger than flattery.

"If you witnessed Juan Padilla's murder and somebody is trying to keep you from testifying, that's a felony," Jessup said. It was one of the possibilities I'd considered. Another was Four O payback time. "We'll arrest whoever it is, and that person won't bother you anymore."

Cheyanne wasn't buying it. Her response was, "I can't tell you."

"Where did the assault take place?" Jessup asked.

"I don't remember exactly. Somewhere on the ditch."

Jessup probed gently, Cheyanne answered reluctantly, revealing little more than she had to me. The detective asked if Cheyanne would help them find the person who had injured her, but Cheyanne said she couldn't do that. When Jessup had finished, she asked if Cheyanne had anything she wanted to say.

"Yes," Cheyanne replied. "I want to plead guilty to the murder of Juan Padilla."

Jessup looked to me for confirmation, since a statement blurted out by a thirteen-year-old girl would not be admissible in court. The time had come to make it official. "My client wishes to plead guilty to Section Thirty-Two-Three, manslaughter," I said.

"Are you sure?" Jessup asked.

"I'm sure," Cheyanne answered.

"I'm going to put you in the D Home, then, and present your plea to the DA's office."

"Go ahead," Cheyanne said. She slumped down in her chair. Her hair fell over her face, and I couldn't see if her expression was one of despair or relief.

When I got to my office I did some slumping of my own, so much so that in the middle of the afternoon Anna knocked on the door and asked if she could get me a coffee or something.

"Thanks anyway," I said, my theory being that when shit happens you get over it faster if you get into it deeper. If you have to feel rotten, you might as well feel good and rotten.

"If Saia does accept her plea it'll only be two years in the Girls' School, right?" Anna said.

"Probably." It wasn't the length of the sentence that bothered me, it was the enormity of the crime— that plus the ages of the victim and my client. Psychologically Cheyanne could be dragging a rotting corpse around her neck for the rest of her life. And there was the other thing. "If she didn't do it and Saia accepts her plea, that'll mean the real killer goes free."

"If it wasn't her, then it was a gang member. They'll duke it out." She paused. "You sure you don't want something to drink?"

"How 'bout a Coke?"

"You got it," Anna said.

When Saia called me an hour later, I'd gotten enough of a buzz on to start drawing diamonds down the side of my legal pad.

"I have a report on my desk that says your client was assaulted," he began.

"My client was assaulted."

"The kind of wounds she had could have been self-inflicted."

"You didn't see how terrified she was when she showed up at my door."

"Terrified of her own self. There's a police report on file saying your client tried to commit suicide three years ago by cutting her wrists with a broken soda bottle. Did you know that?"

"Sure." I was lying, but what the hell, it wasn't the first time Saia had ever been lied to. I had stopped drawing diamonds and started drawing loops.

"She could have cut her face in the same way. The cuts were shallow and the marks weren't inconsistent with those left by a sharp piece of glass."

"You think a pretty thirteen-year-old girl is going to cut her own face?"

"Why not?"

"She had no motive to inflict wounds on herself, Anthony."

"How about this one? She's trying to get out of a bad family situation and into three square meals a day, Nintendo and phone privileges in the D Home."

"She is under suicide watch, I hope."

"She is."

"Maybe it was payback time, Anthony. Did you consider that?"

"Naah, if gangbangers were after a payback they wouldn't have given her those rinky-dinky wounds. They'd have killed her. I'd suspect Ron Cade, except that his alibi for the night of Padilla's murder has turned out to be solid."

"The one that came from the tennis player?"

"Right. He lost in the tournament, by the way."

"Too bad. So what's the alibi?"

"That Cade was watching a video at the tennis player's home in the Country Club area the night of the murder. He's a clean-cut kid, an athlete, a student at the Academy and he's standing by Cade's story. The father is a lawyer who swears his kid is telling the truth."

"Anybody I know?"

"Probably. The guy's a pompous asshole, if you ask me."

That didn't narrow the field much. "Are you going to tell me who?"

"No."

"How does your tennis player compare to your witness?"

"He'd hold up better in court. The witness is a punk."

"You going to tell me who he is now?"

"No."

"You do have somebody out looking for the crime scene and witnesses to my client's assault?" I asked.

"Of course. Your client claims she's in too much pain to go with them."

"Those are nasty wounds she has." One possibility Saia hadn't mentioned was that if the wounds were self-inflicted, the motive had been remorse. "Why don't you call me back when you've completed your investigation?" I asked him.

"Will do," he replied. "We'll hold her in protective custody for a few days until the investigation's complete."

"Good," I said.

After work I went home, picked up the Ziploc bag of grass and went out looking for the crime scene myself. I started at Mirador and walked south along the Chapuzar Lateral, entering a maze of water, weeds and deception. There are places along the ditch banks where you can see the Wind Woman's Mountain, Sandia Peak. And there are places where if you stopped and listened long enough you might hear or see La Llorona and her lost children. There are other places where you see nothing but cottonwoods and five-foot-tall weeds. I didn't have to go far to find the circle of yellow police tape that was getting to be a familiar sight in the hood. At the crime scene weeds had been flattened, crushed and shaped by bodies, but that was the only sign of struggle. Whatever blood had been spilled here had gone on to the crime lab. The site backed up against the ditch embankment and was shaded by a cottonwood. When I stood still I could hear the water lapping gently at the banks. It was a peaceful spot, sung to by water, shaded by the cottonwood. Today it resembled a nest more than the scene of an assault. There were enough crushed weeds to make it appear to me that more than one person had been here, but I wasn't an expert. I took out my bag and compared my grass to the bent and broken blades on the ground. They were identical in shape, texture and their straw color.

I turned around and looked at the back of the houses facing Mirador. There were several long narrow fields between the crime scene and the dwellings— fingers reaching for the water in the ditch. It was only a short walk down the Chapuzar Lateral to my place or to Cheyanne's if you cut diagonally across the fields. I wondered what had enticed or forced her to crawl out her bedroom window and come here in the dark. I also wondered how much investigation I ought to be doing of a crime my client didn't want investigated.

On the west side of the Chapuzar Lateral was a row of two-story town houses trying hard to ignore the fact that they'd been built in New Mexico. A second story in this state is an invitation to sun and wind. No matter how tight the windows, the heat and dust seep in. The height did give the inhabitants a good view of the crime scene, however, and the adjacent fields. I looked up at the second stories, but the blinds were all shut.

Saia called to tell me that Jessup and Donaldson had found the crime scene.

"I know," I said.

"You saw it?"

"Yeah."

"Then you know it was on the Chapuzar Lateral between Mirador and Sunset. There were signs of a struggle. A neighbor heard a dog barking, but nobody saw anybody. The police talked to your client's family, but they weren't any help. Unless she gives us a name, that investigation's going nowhere. The blood sample we got did match your client's type."

"Was any weapon found?"

"No. We got the DNA results back on the bullet you gave me, and you were right—it's the one that killed Juan Padilla."

That didn't surprise me. "Anything new on the gun?"

"No. But there's one more development. A clerk at the Diamond Shamrock on Fourth saw your client running down Ladera alone around midnight the night Juan Padilla was killed."

I'd reached the place I'd been heading, but now that I'd gotten there it felt like a drained dry ditch, a rut with all the life sucked out. "Are you willing to accept my client's plea now?"

"I am under a lot of pressure to indict somebody. I'm willing to run it by a Juvenile Court judge."

"And if the judge accepts it? She pled guilty, Anthony. She says it was an accident. She's cooperating. She's showing remorse. Will you agree to no attempt to get consecutive terms?"

"Assuming she behaves herself in the D Home."

"Assuming."

Something—me or Detective Jessup or the plight of my client—had touched Saia's stony heart and made him say, "Yes."

On my way home from work I stopped at the Diamond Shamrock to buy a quart of milk and fill up on gas. It was late enough that whoever had this shift might still be working at midnight. I waited while the guy at the counter paid for his lottery tickets and the guy behind him paid for his gas. The clerk looked like she could handle herself on an oil rig or in a convenience store. She wore jeans and a plaid shirt. Her face was rough, her shoulders broad, her hair a gray and blonde mix. The store had cleared out, and I hoped it would stay that way long enough for me to find out what I wanted to know. I put my milk on the counter.

"How you doin' this evening?" she asked in a pleasant enough voice.

"Pretty good, and you?"

"Not too bad." She rang up the price of the milk.

I searched in my purse for the money and handed over a five-dollar bill. "Do you work this shift on weekends?"

"I do."

"Were you here the night Juan Padilla was killed?"

"Yup." Her voice was still friendly, but her eyes turned wary. Her fingers remained on the register.

"Would you be willing to tell me what you saw and heard?"

"You mind telling me why you want to know?"

"I'm a lawyer and I'm representing one of the suspects."

That seemed to satisfy her. She handed me my change and told me what she had observed. "I didn't hear the gunshot. I saw that little blonde girl who lives on Mirador. I don't know her name, but she comes in here sometimes. She ran by here all alone around midnight."

"Did she have anything in her hand?"

"Not that I saw. She's your client?" I heard someone coming into the store behind me and could see the clerk shift her attention over my shoulder to the new customer. Awareness is critical when you're working in a convenience store.

"Yeah."

"You have my sympathy," she said.

11

In the morning I went to see Cheyanne at the D Home, a cement compound on Second Street whose grounds are guarded by floodlights and a ten-foot-tall chain-link fence topped by razor wire. I had to go through the electronic gate and three doors before I was able see my client. Some juvenile offenders consider this place a dungeon, others a sanctuary; it depends on where and what they're coming from. The Four O's were bound to have members inside, and I was worried about what they might do to my client. I was relieved to see that she had no new wounds and the old ones were starting to heal. Her bruises had turned into a rainbow of muted colors. The swelling had gone down and I could see her eyes again. She had clean bandages on her cuts. Her hair had been washed and brushed. I'd been expecting to find her anxious and scared, but she was calmer than I'd seen her. Home might not be such a bad word for this place. It was a structure that could protect her from herself and others.

"It looks like you're doing all right," I said.

"It's not so bad in here. I have phone privileges, at least, and I don't have to be around my mother and Leo."

"Leo doesn't have anything to do with your being in here, does he?" I could think of a number of ways in which Leo might have influenced this outcome.

"Naah."

"Has anybody been harassing you?"

"No."

"Have you seen your mother?"

"Yeah." She stared at her clenched hands. I was hoping she'd make a gesture that would open them up. "I wanted my mother to bring Miranda, but they won't let her in here. She has to go back to the school anyway. They found out I'm the one that took her."

"Did you and your mother talk?"

"I guess." Cheyanne shrugged and threw up her hands. "She didn't yell at me, anyway."

It was a step in the right direction. Cheyanne put

her hands in her lap palms-up, enabling me to see what I'd been looking for. Slender scars floated on her wrist like silvery fish. The scars were almost buried in the creases where her hand met her wrist— one reason I hadn't noticed them earlier. "The deputy district attorney told me you tried to commit suicide three years ago," I said.

She nodded and hid her hands under the table.

"Why?"

"I was mad."

"At what?"

"My mother and Leo."

"You're not thinking about doing it again, are you?"

"No. It was dumb. I was just a kid then."

"I went to the place where you were assaulted," I told her. "The police had cleaned it up and taken away the bloody grass. The only blood they found was your type, and they didn't find a weapon. Saia suggested you might have injured yourself."

Cheyanne brought her hands up and touched the bandage on her forehead. "You think I'd cut my own face? No way!"

"You weren't feeling guilty about Juan, were you?"

"No. I mean, yes. I feel guilty all the time, but I wouldn't cut my own face because of it. What is it going to take to make that guy believe me?"

"I think you've succeeded. Ron Cade came up with an alibi. The DNA came back on the bullet, and it is the one that killed Juan Padilla. The clerk at Diamond Shamrock saw you run by there around midnight on the night Juan was killed. You will be arraigned before Juvenile Court Judge John Joseph tomorrow. He will decide whether or not to accept your plea."

"What do I wear?" She was dressed in her baggy blue D Home shirt and pants.

"What you're wearing now."

"Will I get two years?"

"That won't be decided at the arraignment. All you do now is answer the charges. Either the judge believes you or he doesn't. If he does believe you, you'll be sentenced later. How well you behave while you're in here is important. If you're a model detainee, Saia has agreed not to ask for consecutive sentences." Two years was long enough for people to get out of town, get killed or forget. In two years Cheyanne would be only fifteen years old. Young enough to start a new life. Young enough to get into a lot more trouble. Far too young to have a murder hanging around her neck.

"I'll be good," she promised.

"The judge will be impressed if you show remorse in the courtroom."

"No problem. Every time I think about Juan it

makes me want to cry." Her hands were in her lap again and she squeezed them tight.

"It would help if you showed the judge some respect. When you speak to him, call him Your Honor."

"Okay."

"You can still recant if you want to," I said. "It's not too late." But we seemed to be on an express train headed for one destination.

"What does recant mean?"

"Change your story."

She shook her head and her hair fell across her face. "I don't want to change my story."

"You shouldn't keep all your feelings to yourself, Cheyanne."

"I won't."

"Everybody needs someone to talk to."

"I know."

"What was it that got you out of the trailer? You had to know it was a dangerous move."

"That was it."

"What?"

She flipped her hair back and looked me in the eye. "I needed to talk to somebody," she said.

When I left the D Home I waited for the light at Griegos to change and for the northbound traffic to clear before I pulled into the turn lane, the island in the middle of Second Street with curved arrows pointing east toward the D Home and west toward the river. The traffic lights had the effect of gates in a waterway controlling the rate of flow. There were two lanes heading north and two south, both full of potential weapons and victims. From my island in the middle of the street I glanced at the Sandias while waiting for the southbound traffic to clear. The last vehicle before my opening was a pickup truck with two girls inside whose teased hairdos filled the cab. I tightened my grip on the steering wheel and prepared to turn. The truck was no surprise to me; I'd known it was coming. But my reaction startled the women. Thinking I was going to cut in front of them, they began screaming and swearing, two big-haired women on a bad hair day. Road rage in Albucrazy can get you killed in a minute. I know better than to respond, but my middle finger was itchy and before I could stop myself I'd flipped them the bird.

On my way home from work that night I passed the trailer. Sonia's car was gone, but Leo's truck was parked out front. Danny was riding his bike in loops around the yard. Leo came out the door cradling a soccer ball in his right arm. He waved his free hand when he saw me. I stopped the car and rolled down the window.

"What's happening with Cheyanne?" he asked.

"She's going to be arraigned tomorrow."

"I want to be there."

"Okay."

"Will she stay in the D Home after the arraignment?"

"Probably. If the judge grants bail I suspect it will be high."

He looked around the bare yard. "Not much collateral here."

"True," I said.

Leo tightened his grip on the ball. "Did Cheyanne tell you if anybody's been hassling her? She won't tell her mother anything."

"She says no."

"If you hear she's having any trouble with gang members in there, you let me know."

"All right. You were here the night she was assaulted?"

"Right."

"What was it that got her out of the house? Do you know?"

"It wasn't the phone. Sonia had it disconnected. The TV was on. I didn't hear anybody outside."

"You guys didn't fight, did you?"

"No."

Danny had circled closer, zeroing in on us. He parked next to Leo and put his kickstand down.

"There's a game on," Leo said. "We gotta go." He handed the ball over to Danny.

"Talk to you later," I replied.

When I got to my driveway I stopped to pick up the mail, looked back down the road and saw Leo following Danny toward the rec field next to the Sacred Heart Church where the soccer games were played. Danny rode his bike with the soccer ball in one hand and the handlebars in the other, but it was awkward. The bike weaved back and forth across the road. Danny stopped and waited for his father to catch up. When Leo did, Danny tossed him the ball. Leo bounced it up in the air with his shoulder and caught it in his arms on the way back down.

12

*When a thirteen-year-*old girl is indicted for homicide in Albuquerque, it's a major news event, and the press showed up in full force at the arraignment. The reporters waiting outside Juvenile Court wanted to get a statement from me, but I had nothing to say. Inside the courtroom the cameras were set up and the Four O's were waiting, wearing black t's with smile now, cry later masks on the front and Old English letters on the back that read Juan Padilla, RIP.

An invisible line divided the courtroom down the middle. Juan's mourners crowded into one side of it and Cheyanne's supporters took the other. There were only four people on Cheyanne's side: Sonia, Leo, Danny and Patricia. It was more than a lot of juvenile offenders had. Sonia wore a short black skirt and a black western shirt with turquoise trim and silver tips on the collar. Her hands tugged nervously at the skirt. Leo wore his repairman's shirt, as if he intended to go back to the job the minute this was over. His left side was turned away from the Four O's, shielding Danny, who stood to his right. Danny was jittery as a cricket and Leo put his hand on his shoulder to settle him down. He had the slicked-back hair of a junior gang member, but his mother hadn't let him dress the part. He wore straight-legged jeans and a plain t-shirt. Patricia had on a green dress and a lot of makeup. Her curls tumbled down her back. Today she was fourteen going on twenty-one. She was the only one in the courtroom who dared to stare across the aisle.

The other side of the room was dominated by gangsters. They wore full pants and had their hair clipped close to their heads, trying their best to scare us more than we scared them. The Four O's didn't have to look tough to convince me. These boys could well have been to more funerals than they had birthday parties, which would give them an older person's perspective that death is the place where you go to reconnect with friends and family who have already passed on. The gang members were a dark cloud on

Juan's side of the courtroom. In front of them sat the women: a mother, aunts, sisters, a grandmother. All the grown men in this family appeared to be absent or dead. An old woman looked up from the soggy handkerchief she clutched and her eyes met mine. She had the long, furrowed face of a hound. Her white hair was slipping out of its bun. Her legs were thick as tree trunks. Her mournful brown eyes said Juan had been more than a gang member—he'd been a hope for the future. There was no accusation or threat in her look—only loss—so I couldn't justify myself by getting angry or defensive.

Cheyanne didn't look at the Padillas or the Four O's or her own family either when she entered. She wore her blue D Home uniform with the numbers on the back. Her arms still showed the marks of the assault. Her movements were sluggish. She wore no makeup and she'd wiped off the last of the blue nail polish. Her hair had been brushed until the curls had fallen out. She'd peeled off her bandages and her stitches were visible, giving her the sewn-together look of a rag doll. I wasn't sure looking like a waif would convince anyone she was guilty of murder, but I could have been underestimating the weariness and experience of Juvenile Court Judge John Joseph, who was known for his unpredictability. The way he reacted could depend on whether his breakfast had agreed with him or whether he'd experienced road rage on his way to work. Cheyanne didn't cry as she stood before him, but she did have the slouch of a victim deep in depression and the clenched hands of a wrongdoer full of remorse.

When she appeared, the gangbangers looked away in unison, like a bunch of raw recruits under the command of a drill sergeant. But I couldn't tell who was giving the orders; no one stood out as bigger or meaner or older. One guy wore a black baseball cap turned backward and a jacket with white stitching across the front. Maybe it was him. He was better-looking than the other gangbangers, with small features, pale and striking eyes. Sometimes good looks are authority enough, but I didn't know if that would cut it among these tough guys.

The eyes that had avoided Cheyanne glared at me as I approached the bench to face Judge Joseph, but that's my job, to absorb the anger and the heat. Saia stood beside me, and if he was feeling any heat he didn't let it show. His hair was slick and smooth. His clothes were deeply rumpled.

Judge Joseph glared at my client over the top of his dime-store reading glasses, and his fine white hair shimmied with static. He'd been on the bench for years and had seen a whole lot of kids in trouble. He'd seen girls who'd killed and girls who'd been assaulted. He'd seen pretty girls, ugly girls, innocent girls, guilty girls, but it was unlikely he'd seen many girls who lived in harmony with their parents and he'd undoubtedly seen some whose parents hadn't even shown up. The judge read off the charges against my client and asked her if I had explained the charges and the consequences.

Cheyanne nodded.

"Don't nod, young lady," he barked. "Answer me."

"Yes," Cheyanne mumbled.

"What?" The judge cupped his hand to his ear.

"Yes, Your Honor."

"You are charged with a capital offense. Do you understand what that means?"

"It means I killed somebody." Cheyanne paused as if trying to remember something. Maybe it was my admonition to show remorse. "I'm very sorry for my actions, Your Honor," she continued.

"Why is that?" queried the judge.

"I shot Juan Padilla and caused his family pain and suffering."

"What were the circumstances of the shooting?"

"I . . . I was holding the gun in my hand. The gun went off."

"Did you act alone?"

"Yes."

"Was it your intent to shoot Juan Padilla?" He stared down at her from the height of the bench, making my client appear very small, very young and very scared.

She shook her head. "No. It was an accident, Your Honor."

"Where did you get the weapon?"

"I found it."

The judge took his eyes off Cheyanne for a moment and appraised me. "Are you satisfied with your legal representation, young lady?" he asked her.

"Yes," my client answered.

"And with your guilty plea?"

She'd had the option of taking an Alford Plea, which doesn't admit guilt, only that the prosecutor can prove guilt, but that hadn't been my client's wish. My client had wanted to stand up before the judge and the Padillas and plead guilty. The time had come to do so.

"Yes, Your Honor," she whispered.

The judge stared at her for a long time. He closed his eyes briefly and when he opened them he said, "I am taking your plea under advisement and will schedule a hearing when I have made my decision."

"When will that be, Your Honor?" asked Cheyanne.

"When I have given the matter due consideration," he snapped. Considering the age of the defendant, Judge Joseph would be expected to take a long, hard look at this case, which would include reports from a psychiatrist and a probation officer. But his sour expression indicated he'd made up his mind.

He set bail at an amount Sonia Moran couldn't possibly meet and remanded Cheyanne to the D Home until the plea hearing. Maybe he thought the D Home would be the best place for her. Maybe he thought she would be a menace out on the street. He pounded his gavel and dismissed us.

Juan's women sobbed while the attendant led Cheyanne—hiding behind her hair—back to the D Home. It was all the state could do, but it would never be enough for the Padillas. Leo hurried Sonia and Danny outside. The newscasters headed for the door and the cameramen began hauling away their equipment. For them the drama was over.

I watched Patricia step across the divide and walk up to the guy in the black hat, who was talking to one of his homeboys. His back was to me and I could read the inscription on his turned-backward hat. BROWN POWER, it said in white Old English letters. The guy didn't know Patricia was behind him until she tapped him on the shoulder. He spun around like he was getting ready to take a swing, but when he saw it was Patricia he stopped himself, looked her up and down and smiled smoothly.

"Looking baaad today, Patricia," he said. "Real bad."

"Take your breath away," she replied.

"Don't count on it." His smile turned cold and hard.

One of Juan's young women, a girlfriend or a sister, grabbed Patricia's arm. "Your girlfriend's gonna rot in jail, bitch," she hissed.

"Chill out, Laura," Black Hat said.

Patricia shook the girl off, turned her back and walked away.

Black Hat held the girl in check until Patricia was out the door. I'd been standing by the bench watching and the girl turned toward me. "That goes for you, too," she said.

"Just doing my job," I replied.

"It's a hoe's job."

Whores get paid better than me, I thought, but I let my feet do the talking. I walked out of the courtroom, down the hallway, out the door and onto the street, where I encountered the cloud of smoke that hovers outside every professional building. My buddy and adversary, Anthony Saia, was standing in the middle of it puffing on a Camel.

"Give me a hit," I said.

"Just one?"

"That's all."

He handed over the cigarette. "Remember when these things used to be called coffin nails?" he asked me.

"I remember." I took one deeply satisfying drag, coughed and handed the cigarette back. Saia finished it off, dropped it to the sidewalk and rubbed it out. Then we walked to the corner, where we intended to go our separate ways—he back to the DA's office, me to the underground parking lot where I'd left my Nissan. "Don't let it get to you," he told me while we walked.

"It's not," I replied, pulling my dark glasses out of my purse. The sun and the wind were making their presence felt in the canyons of downtown, causing me to put on my sunglasses and making Anthony Saia squint. One side of the street was in sunlight. The other was in shadow. Both sides were feeling the wind, which picked up trash and swirled it around.

Saia did not accept my denial. "What's the problem?" he asked.

"It's hard to watch a teenage client plead guilty to manslaughter." And not that easy to confront the friends and family of a fifteen-year-old victim.

"Happens every day," he said.

"Not to my clients."

"That's because you've been going for the big-buck negligence cases." He laughed.

"Ha, ha," I replied. "Cheyanne will stay on suicide watch, I hope."

"I'll look into it. If you ask me, she's better off in the D Home than she is in her own home if the mother's hanging out with Chuy Ortega." The wind tugged at Saia's hair and whipped mine across my face.

"Do you mean Leo?" I asked.

"Yeah."

"He's the father of Sonia's son."

"When I read the police report for the night your client was assaulted I didn't realize I knew him. There are a lot of Ortegas out there. Your client pled guilty and refused to cooperate in the assault investigation, so it went no further. I didn't put it together until I saw Ortega in court today. I knew him by his gang name of Chuy. He was a violent son of a bitch back then."

"What'd he do?"

"Aggravated battery. I prosecuted him about ten years ago."

"You've been prosecuting that long?"

"That long."

"Maybe you're getting stuck, Anthony."

"Maybe one day a new DA will come along and kick me out. I am getting tired of seeing the same faces over and over again." He looked tired. Squinting was deepening the wrinkles around his mouth and lengthening the bags beneath his eyes.

"How much time did Leo do?" I asked him.

"A year."

"He seems devoted to his son. Maybe being a father has straightened him out."

"It's a tough job," Saia said, "but somebody's got to do it. It's getting to be too much for parents all alone. Maybe Hillary was right when she said it takes a village, only we don't have villages anymore. The city is swallowing them up."

"We do have streets," I said.

"True. Don't go beating yourself up over this case, Neil. If Joseph does accept your client's plea and sends her to the Girls' School, it's not exactly a dungeon."

"There are going to be Four O's or their girl-friends inside who can make it hell for my client if they want to. They were showing their colors in the courtroom."

"I guess we'll find out then whether our justice is their justice, whether they believe your client is guilty or not." The wind had pried one lock of graying hair loose, and it danced across Saia's forehead.

My own hair was blowing into my face. I brushed it away. "Who was the kid in the black hat?" I asked.

"Nolo Serrano. Good-looking kid, huh?"

"Not bad."

"He should have been a movie star or a musician instead of a gangbanger. He plays the guitar and was doing all right with it until he dropped out of school."

"How do you know him? He's not your eye-witness, is he?"

"You're asking me to give up a witness?"

"The case has already been settled, Anthony. My client pled guilty."

"The witness is still a juvenile."

"Then can you tell me if he's not your witness?"

"I told you my witness wasn't a gangbanger, didn't I?"

"That's what you said."

"It's not Serrano. The way I know him is he's been in and out of the system. That kid can charm the bark off a tree or the money out of a lawyer if he wants to. He's not bad, just misdirected."

A woman was coming down the street wearing high heels and a power suit that made mine look like it was fifteen years old. She held a bottle of designer water by the neck and she smiled at Saia.

"Could that be the new lady friend?" I asked.

Saia slicked the errant strand of hair into place. "That's Jennifer." She did look impressively fit, a lot fitter than Anthony Saia. This was not a lawyer who intended to be clerking for long. "You want to meet her?" Saia asked.

I wasn't in the mood for Xena, Warrior Princess. I could see what Saia saw in her, but not what she saw in him. World-weariness can be a comfort, but it's not a turn-on—not to me, anyway. "Maybe later. I gotta get back to the office."

"Talk to you later," Saia said.

"Okay," I answered.

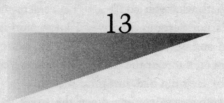

13

*I walked to the under-*ground lot where my Nissan was parked and took the elevator down to Level Three. I don't like parking lots. What woman does? An inside lot is worse than outside, unless it's after dark. The concrete ceiling, the institutional lighting, the shadows under the Broncos and BMWs told me to get in and out fast. Usually I circle the levels until I find a spot that's close to the elevator. I like to have as few vehicles as possible between escape and my Nissan. But today there'd been no close-in spots on any level. Several cars away on Level Three was the best I'd been able to do.

Guilt was at my side when I got on the elevator. The deal I'd made for my client was not justice for the Padillas and maybe not for my client, either. While the elevator descended I took out my key ring, made a fist and inserted the keys between my fingers, not a bad idea when you're entering a parking lot. I got off the elevator, saw that I was the only living thing on Level Three and walked to my car. When I got there and inserted the key in the lock I heard the elevator descending and the door sliding open.

I turned around and saw Nolo Serrano—many women's dark and handsome nightmare—dance through the sliding door. No one is as much trouble as a good-looking guy. I'd lived long enough to know that and to remember when fear took the form of dirty old men. Now it's teenagers who bring on the goose bumps. None of Nolo's homeboys followed him. The door rolled shut, and he and I were alone on Level Three. My right hand went to my purse, reaching automatically for the piece I wasn't packing, hoping Serrano didn't know that.

"Hey!" He held up his hands. "I'm not packin'."

I didn't think he'd come down here to pick up his car. So what was it? And why was he alone? I didn't intend to let Nolo Serrano charm the money out of me. I kept one hand on my keys and the other on my purse. "What do you want?" I asked.

"Just to talk is all. Just want to talk." He boogalooed a little closer. His movements and speech had a quick and nervous rhythm.

"I can hear you fine from where you are." And I could also see how pretty he was, even in the harsh underground light. His pale eyes, fringed by thick black lashes, danced with amusement. His hat framed his face in black. The white scar that I'd noticed on his jacket turned out to be an embroidered zipper.

"Okay, okay." He tried to stand still, but he was too wired. He did a little rubber-soled dance while we talked.

"Laura, she shouldn't have called you a hoe. You were just doing your job. It's a tough job, I know. But you and Cheyanne, you did the right thing. She did the crime, hey, she should do the time."

"Just as long as she's not doing more than her time," I said.

"She'll do better on the inside if she stays cool, keeps her mouth shut. There's some bad people in the D Home, and what you say there can be used against you. Has anybody been bothering her?"

"No. Let's keep it that way."

"No problem. The Four O's inside, they won't hassle Cheyanne."

"How do you know that?"

"I'm the leader," said Nolo. He smiled the smile of an actor who wins an Oscar, a mystery writer who gets the Edgar, a lawyer who gets to argue before the Supreme Court. At sixteen or seventeen years old he'd achieved all he'd ever dreamed.

"How'd you get the name Nolo?" I asked him.

"First I was Manuel, then Manolo, now I'm Nolo. You get a new name when you rank in." His eyes rolled up until the whites were visible under the pupils. "How'd you know my name was Nolo?"

"Deputy DA Saia told me."

"That guy's a lawyer, too, right?"

"Right."

"How do you like being a lawyer?"

"It's okay."

"Maybe that's what I'll be when I grow up." He smiled.

"Maybe," I said, but when I looked into his eyes I saw a boy who'd never grow up.

"Can you explain something to me about lawyers?"

"Try me."

"I see you and that DA in court. You're on one side. He's on the other side. Then when it's over I see you smoking a cigarette together. I see you talking. I see you walking down the street. How can you be enemies on the inside and friends on the outside?"

"That's the way it is in the professional world."

He shook his head. "It's not like that in my

world. Someone's your homeboy or he's not."

No shit, I thought. His world was ruled by hormones, drugs, egos and guns. All lawyers had going for us was ego and an ever-diminishing supply of hormones. It's a crazy society that lets teenagers pack semiautomatics. "Your world is trigger-happy," I said.

"That's the truth."

"I heard you were a musician," I said, changing the subject, hoping to discover more about Nolo Serrano.

"Who told you that?"

"Saia." Nolo's feet continued their restless dance. On the one hand, he didn't like Saia talking about him. On the other hand, any kind of attention had value because it made his name come out. "Were you a musician?"

"Used to be. Used to be."

"The man in my life is a musician."

"What does he play?"

"The accordion."

"I played the guitar."

"Why did you give it up?"

"See this?" He pointed to the zipper embroidered on his jacket. "That means I caught a bullet. That's when I got into gang life. *Mi Vida Loca.* It's the crazy life, but it's my life." He laughed. "You'll be seeing Cheyanne?"

"Right."

"You tell her I'll be watching out for her."

"I'll do that."

"*Bueno.* Gotta go. *Mucho gusto.*"

"*El gusto es mio,*" I said, watching him dance back to the elevator and wondering how long he'd have wings on his feet.

The Kid worked late that night, and by the time he got home I'd had a burrito and a couple of tequilas and gone to bed. He thumped around the house until he tracked me down in the bedroom wearing a pillow over my head. "You're sleeping, chiquita?" he asked.

"Not anymore."

He sat down on the bed beside me and lifted the pillow. "You never go to bed this early."

"It was a bad day."

"You went to court?"

"Yeah."

"What happened?"

"Cheyanne was arraigned."

"You knew that was going to happen, no?"

Count on a man to be reasonable when the problem has nothing to do with reason. "It was worse than I expected. Cheyanne was comatose. Juan's family was grieving and hostile."

"They blame you?"

"Probably."

"It will make them feel better, but after a boy gets in a gang it is already too late for him. I see them come into the shop and I see they are in love with death."

"The zipper embroidered on the jacket means they've been wounded?"

"Right. After that happens they get too tough."

"One of the Four O's who was in the courtroom followed me into the parking garage after the arraignment, but very carefully. I didn't know I was being tagged."

The Kid dropped his hand and sat straight up on the edge of the bed. "Who?"

"Nolo Serrano. Do you know him?"

"I know who he is. He has a Fast Five convertible, red and white, *muy suave.*" Sometimes I heard grudging respect or at least understanding when the Kid talked about gang members, but this time I heard respect for the car, contempt for the driver. "What did that *cholo* want?"

"He says he's the leader of the Four O's. He told me he would make sure nobody hurt Cheyanne in the D Home."

"Why would he do that?"

"I don't know."

"That guy will never last as a leader."

"Why not?"

"He's too pretty. Nobody will respect him. He will have to prove how tough he is over and over again. One day he won't be watching or listening and somebody will kill him," he snapped his fingers, "like that."

"He told me that he'd been shot and after that he got into the gang life. He said he played the guitar, but he gave it up after he was wounded."

"Yeah?" said the Kid. He used to play his accordion in a Norteno band—but he hadn't been doing it lately.

"It seems like he might have had some potential."

"Him?" The Kid sneered.

I changed the subject. "Have you had any luck finding Saia's witness yet?"

"No. You want me to keep looking now that the girl is in prison?"

"Yeah," I said.

The night got off to a smooth start, but later on it turned rough. I drifted in and out of sleep. A day that should have provided closure had only raised questions. A restless wind mirrored my scattered mind. A tree limb skated across the skylight, the dogs in the hood howled and barked, my neighbor's motion detector light flickered on and off. There were plenty

of images that could have disturbed my dreams—
handsome teens, ugly teens, rumpled prosecutors,
snarling judges in flapping black robes—but the
image that haunted me most was the grandmother's
dark eyes.

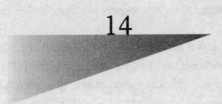

14

In the morning I passed the trailer on my way to work, saw Sonia's car parked in the yard and pulled in beside it. The scratches and dings on the bumper and the hood marked her vehicle as a junker, although the frame around her license plate read THOROUGHBRED TOYOTA.

"Come on in," she yelled when I knocked on the door. "I knew it was you. I saw your car pull up." She was sitting on the sofa smoking a cigarette and cradling the doll Miranda in her arms.

"How are you doing?" I asked.

"Gettin' by."

"Cheyanne told me the school wants Miranda back."

"They've been calling me at work. I'll take her over there today." She looked down at the doll. "Cheyanne was a real happy baby, always smiling and laughing. How in the hell did she turn out to be a murderer? Can you answer me that?"

"No."

"Would it have made any difference if I'd stayed home with her? If I hadn't worked nights? If I'd cuddled her more?" She stared at me through a filter of smoke.

"I don't know," I said. I wasn't anybody to be giving mother/daughter advice, but I did it anyway. "It might help if you weren't always turning Danny into the good child and Cheyanne into the bad."

She took a deep drag and exhaled. "I do that?"

"Yeah. Talk to Cheyanne. Tell her you're human. That you never took mother lessons. That you make mistakes. You can still change things."

"I worry about what will happen to her in there. . . ."

So did I. Nolo Serrano's promises hadn't changed that.

"I worry about what's gonna happen when she gets out," Sonia continued.

"There are plenty of cases of people who commit bad crimes and go on to make something of their lives," I said. "Anthony Saia told me Leo did time."

"A year," Sonia replied, rubbing her cigarette out

in the ashtray. "I met him right after he got out. He was tough as nails, but he learned something inside. He finished his GED, started pumping iron, learned to manage his anger—that's what his probation officer called it—anger management. When Leo gets pissed off now, weightlifting calms him down. We had Danny, he got a job. He's been a good father to Danny. You watch them on the soccer field sometime if you don't believe me. He'd do anything to keep Danny out of the gangs. Leo and I split up after Danny was born. When we tried to get back together later it was hard because Cheyanne was older and she was jealous and she didn't have a father of her own."

"Is that when she tried to commit suicide?"

"How'd you know about that?" The eyes behind the smokescreen turned wary.

"Saia told me."

"How'd he find out?"

"The police filed a report on the suicide attempt."

"Oh, yeah, a cop came to the hospital. Does that Saia know everything there is to know about us? Ain't there no privacy left in this town?"

"Not after you get into the system."

"I thought Cheyanne was trying to get attention. She and Leo fought all the time. That's one reason we don't live together now. Did you ever meet a kid who got along with a stepparent?"

"Not yet." She wouldn't like what I had to say next, but I had to say it. "It's an explosive situation when there's a guy and a young girl sharing a house."

Her hand, which had been reaching for another cigarette, stopped in midair. "What are you saying?"

"Cheyanne has a lot of resentment toward Leo. Leo has a temper. He has a record. They were alone together the night she got beat up." I shouldn't be thinking about that night anymore, but it wouldn't let go of me.

Sonia struck a match, lit the cigarette and blew out the match with the cigarette dangling from her lip. "What kind of a mother do you think I am? You think I'd have a guy in my house who'd mess with my daughter? They weren't alone anyway. Danny was here."

True. But Danny was nine years old.

"If you knew Leo better you wouldn't be making accusations like that."

Maybe. I'd gone about as far as I could down that highway, so I changed directions. "Did you ever meet a kid named Manuel Serrano who calls himself Nolo?"

"I don't think so. What does he look like?"

"He's around sixteen or seventeen. He wears a black hat that says BROWN POWER, and he has a zipper embroidered on his jacket."

"I don't remember him."

"He stopped me after the arraignment and told me he'd look after Cheyanne in the D Home."

"How's he gonna do that?"

"He says he's the leader of the Four O's."

"If he says he can protect her, I'm not gonna say no." She reached into her pocket, pulled out a roll of bills and handed them to me. "I did good last night," she said. "I'll pay you more when I can. All right?"

"All right."

She yawned. "Gettin' past my bedtime."

And past time for me to go to work. I put the bills in my purse and told Sonia I'd let her know when the next hearing was scheduled.

While we waited for the psychiatric evaluation and for Judge Joseph to make his decision, I fell back into the real estate and divorce routine, which didn't seem so bad compared to a case as ambiguous as Cheyanne Moran's. Divorce may seem ambiguous to the participants, but to the observer it isn't—especially when you've seen as many as I have. Cheyanne was as comfortable in the D Home as could be expected. Actually, she seemed more comfortable than I would have expected. When I told her I'd met Nolo Serrano and that he'd said he was looking out for her, her response was to study her bitten-down fingernails.

"Do you know him?" I asked.

"I've met him."

"Do you think he can make good on his promise?"

"No one's been hassling me so far except for that psychiatrist. That guy wants to know everything."

"Are you cooperating?"

"Sort of."

"Sort of is not good enough. You have to work with him."

"Okay, okay."

Cheyanne was looking better. The swelling had receded from her eyes and the colors had faded. The cuts on her face were healing. The stitches had been taken out, so she didn't have that rag doll look anymore, but it was too early to tell whether she'd have permanent scars. If she did, the scars would be close enough to the hairline that they could be concealed—if she chose to conceal them.

When I'd said what I had to say, the guards took her back to her room and let me out through the triple doors and electronic gate. The usual collection of tough guys was standing by the entrance showing their colors.

Cheyanne was surviving in the D Home. The Kid and I were getting by in my home, making the adjustments it takes to live together: deciding when to get up, what to watch on television, divvying up the chores. We could tolerate the same level of messiness, so cleaning wasn't a conflict. I did as little gardening as possible, he did none. We both chased the gray cat away. He liked baseball (and *Walker, Texas Ranger*), I liked crime shows (except for *Walker, Texas Ranger*), but the different types of programs we liked hardly ever aired concurrently. Food was no problem; we both liked it hot. Cooking and dishwashing were easy. We got takeout and the plastic dishes and utensils went in the garbage. The Kid didn't care for the garbage detail, so I walked it down the driveway every week. The tradeoff was he made the coffee and he got up early so that I woke to the smell of coffee brewing. Usually he was gone by the time I got out of bed, but that was okay; neither of us were morning talkers. We both worked hard—me with my mouth and my brain, he with his hands. Some people might think that made us incompatible, but I didn't feel that the fact that his work wasn't verbal made him inferior or dumb. I'd never thought there was that much status in being a lawyer; half the population might admire you, but the other half hates your guts. To me it's attitude that counts, and the Kid's attitude toward work was good. We didn't get as far as mentioning the big C word—commitment—but were working on the little one—consideration—which helps if you're trying to live together. Life was still a dangerous place, but it was gentler when he was around.

Occasionally I saw Danny ride by on his bike. I didn't see Sonia, Leo or Patricia, and Tabatoe stayed away, frightened off by the gray cat.

Anna and her boyfriend, known to me as the stereo king for the power of his car speakers, were drag-racing down the breakup road, playing chicken on the highway of love. This guy had never learned anger management, and he vented his rage by driving by the office and pounding the pavement with his speakers, or by calling and hanging up if I answered, yelling if Anna did. That drama kept the office from becoming too boring.

One night on my way home from the Women's Bar Association meeting I saw a nearly full moon climbing over the back of the Sandias. The Kid's truck was parked in my driveway, but I wasn't ready to go home or to bed, so I kept on driving. There are times when driving comes easier than falling asleep. I headed north on Fourth Street past the old adobes, the new subdivisions and the church at Alameda. I watched the moon rise and listened for what it had to say. In New Mexico the moon speaks. There was a box in my glove compartment that spoke, too, in a raspy, seductive voice, but I focused on the moon and ignored it.

I passed El Pinto restaurant, which seemed to be

expanding at the same astronomical rate as the city.
Where Fourth Street turned to Roy and headed east
toward the Sandia Casino, I went north on 85
through Sandia Pueblo. Sandia is the place where
urban sprawl becomes the big empty. One side of
Roy is city, the other is land. Albucrazy doesn't peter
out into suburbia—it ends at the Sandia Pueblo on
the north, the Isleta Pueblo on the south, the mountains and the Cibola National Forest on the east. The
only way it can expand is west of the Rio Grande,
and that's what it's doing. Maybe the Petroglyph
National Monument would form a barrier on that
side. Maybe not. Still, you could go fifteen minutes
in any direction and be out of the city, which was
what made living in it possible for me.

The moonglow was so bright that I could see the
cottonwoods beside the river and the Sandia pueblo
church nestled on the east side of the road. The
mountains took on definition from the moon. There
was a place out here that kids called the twilight zone
where they went to take drugs and spin their cars
out. A jet crossed the sky from east to west, leaving a
contrail that turned luminous under the light of the
moon. At first it was a tight, bright line, then it began
to widen and dissipate.

I didn't pass a single car as I drove through Sandia. I continued north until I reached the village of
Bernalillo, where I stopped at the Range Cafe in the

old monastery. It was too late for the cafe to be open, but I wanted to turn around and take a good look at the sky. The first contrail had faded to a chalk line, but another jet was crossing from north to south. The moon was higher now, and it turned this contrail into a long dark shadow.

15

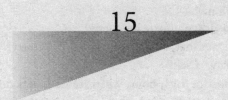

A few days later, when
I came back from lunch with a pack of Nicorette
gum, Anna told me that Anthony Saia had called.

"What did he want?" I asked. That my client was
having problems—or causing problems—in the D
Home was always a possibility. If that was the case, I
wasn't sure I wanted to be hearing about it from
Anthony Saia. A second possibility was that Judge
Joseph's decision had come down.

"He didn't say," Anna replied.

I went into my office and dialed Saia's number.
"Qué pasa?" I asked when he picked up the phone.

"Can you come over here?"

"Why?"

"There's something I want to show you."

I bit the bullet. "My client's not having problems in the D Home, is she?"

"Nope."

"Has Joseph made his ruling?"

"It's not that, either. How about five-thirty?"

"Okay," I said.

It was the rush hour, when traffic meets downtown construction and comes to a halt. I negotiated my way to Saia's office through the orange barrel slalom, doing my best not to swear or wave my middle finger or give any outward sign of impatience.

Saia—who hadn't had to drive anywhere—was sitting at his desk looking more relaxed than I'd seen him in a while. "Pleasure to see you, Neil," he said, standing up and offering his hand.

"You too," I replied. "What's up?"

A shiny black videocassette lay on top of the pile on his desk. The cassette was labeled, but I couldn't read what it said from where I sat.

"Porn?" I asked. The thought of Saia caught in the act with Xena, Warrior Princess, passed through my mind, but I attached wings to that thought and sent it flying. I didn't think he and Xena together was a video Saia would want to share with me. And Saia obviously intended to share this one; he was already loading it into the VCR.

"Not exactly," he replied. "You know Harry's, the scuzzy bar on Grande?"

"The one with the sign that says it's the hottest wet spot in town?"

"That's the one. We've long suspected them of prostitution, serving minors, dealing drugs, selling liquor after hours, you name it. The police conducted a raid last week, and they've been working their way through the surveillance tape. It took a while for this to make its way to my desk."

He clicked the remote and started the black-and-white video. The foreground was in focus. The background was gray and grainy. The date and time appeared in the upper-right-hand corner. It was after hours, although the place was still occupied.

The surveillance camera focused on two teenage boys sitting at the bar talking, laughing and drinking. One of them popped the tab off a crack vial and filled a pipe. He started to pass it over to the other guy, but then he laughed and pulled it back, holding out for more money or for something else or just being a pain in the ass. I recognized the seller (or giver) as Ron Cade. His hair was blonde and curly and he wore an earring in one ear. He had high cheekbones and even features. But when he laughed I could see what the police sketch and photos hadn't revealed— his mouth was a pit, his teeth were rotten and crooked. Someone should have given him braces and caps, but no one had, although this was supposedly a kid from a well-to-do family. Maybe his teeth had gotten broken too often to fix.

The other boy was about the same age as Cade, but clean-cut: no body piercing, baggy clothes, weird hairdo or turned-backward hat. He had bangs that fell across his forehead, an unblemished face, and the slender build of a tennis player. This boy looked as if he'd spent more time at the country club than he had on the street. He could be a kid who'd been showered with attention, a boy of whom much had been expected, maybe too much, because his hands trembled when he reached for the pipe. His expression changed from eager to desperate as Cade yanked the pipe away. Cade held onto it until the boy was willing to beg. Only after he mouthed the word "please" did Cade hand the pipe back. The guy smoked the crack cocaine, which quickly elevated his mood. Cade gave him some more vials and he gave Cade a high five. Some kind of deal appeared to have been consummated. I thought I knew what it was, because the date that appeared in the corner of the frame was the same day my client had been arraigned.

"That's the tennis player who provided Cade's alibi?" I asked.

"Right."

"A crackhead. No wonder he lost the match. Is this the payoff for the alibi?"

"Looks like it. The date, you may have noticed, is the date of your client's arraignment."

"I noticed. Can you tell me the kid's name now?"

"I'll tell you once I prove his alibi is false. All right?" The names of witnesses were cards that Saia liked to hold close to his vest.

"All right." I didn't know the guy's name yet, but I knew he was a student at Albuquerque Academy and the son of a prominent attorney known to be a pompous ass, the price some attorneys are more than willing to pay for success. "Whoever he is, Daddy's not gonna like this," I said.

"Nope."

"His son looked pretty eager for the coke."

"Desperate, if you ask me." Saia pushed the rewind button and the tape wound its way back to the beginning.

"Can't be good for the tennis game."

"I don't think he's been winning lately."

"Does the father know about this tape?"

"Not yet." Saia leaned back in his chair and tapped the tips of his fingers together.

"What was the alibi? This kid was at home watching a video with Cade on the night of the murder?"

"That's right."

"What video?"

"Die Hard 2," Saia said.

"And the father backed Junior up?"

"He said he trusted his son."

"I'd love to be a fly on the wall when you show Daddy the video."

"I'll give you a report." The video had finished rewinding. Saia popped it out and returned it to its place of honor on top of his desk.

"So now you have the son for perjury and drug dealing."

"Don't forget drinking under age."

But I knew he'd drop all the charges if the tennis player would give up Saia's nemesis Ron Cade.

"Will your client recant if I disprove Cade's alibi?" Saia asked me.

"Disprove it and we'll talk," I said.

I didn't have the privilege of sticking to the wall when the tennis player was questioned. Since he was a juvenile, the father was likely to be present in the capacity of either lawyer or father. The police cannot question a juvenile without one or the other. Saia told me that the father was furious and the son was terrified, though he couldn't tell what terrified the son more—the wrath of his father or the prospect of double-crossing Ron Cade. The son confessed that he had manufactured the alibi in exchange for the cocaine, but he said he had no knowledge of Cade's actual whereabouts the night Padilla was shot. He said all he knew was that Cade wasn't with him. Saia didn't press charges. The police released the kid in the custody of his father. He'd be facing anger in the home and terror whenever he went out on the street. Ron Cade and his gang were unlikely to forget that he'd been double-crossed.

"Are you going to tell me the father's name now?" I asked Saia.

"Henry J. O'Brien. You know him?"

"Yeah. You're right. He is a pompous ass. Are you going to bring Ron Cade in?"

"If we can find him," Saia said.

In the morning I went through the gates of the D Home and into the dreary visitor's room once again to tell my client that Ron Cade's phony alibi could open the doors for her. She looked comfortable and rested and might be better off in here than O'Brien Jr. would be on the street. But she had Nolo Serrano looking out for her, and O'Brien would have Ron Cade gunning for him.

"The person who gave Ron Cade an alibi recanted," I told Cheyanne.

"Oh." Cheyanne stared at her fingernails. I'd been hoping for a little more enthusiasm.

"If you'll say Cade assaulted you and made you confess to Juan Padilla's homicide and if you'll testify you saw him shoot Padilla, I'm sure Saia wouldn't charge you with being an accessory. You could be out of here."

She squeezed her hands together and looked down; I was now staring at the top of her head. "I can't do that," she mumbled.

"Are you afraid?"

She nodded.

"Once Cade is in jail, you won't have to worry about him anymore." She might still have been worried about Cade's homeboys. Or she might have been worried about someone else. It was possible that the truth of the Padilla shooting had still not come out. Maybe it was stuck in the mud somewhere in an undredged portion of the ditch.

"I can't. That's all. I'm cool here. Don't worry."

"I'm available if you change your mind," I replied.

She put her hand on top of mine. "I know that," she said.

When I got to the office, I called Saia. "She won't recant," I told him.

"Shit," was his reply.

"She might be more inclined to cooperate if Cade was in custody."

"She's in custody. What's she worried about?"

"The long arm of the gangs."

"We're looking for Cade," Saia said. "That guy can disappear faster than a lizard."

"Maybe he's hiding in a hole in the ground."

"His parents live in the Heights. Who knows where the hell he hangs out."

Now that Cade's alibi was destroyed, the testimony of Saia's witness had become important all over again. "What's happening with your original witness?" I asked him.

"He's sticking by his story. He says he'll never forget. I like that in a witness."

"And you're sure he's not a gang member?" I asked.

"I'm sure," he said.

Often you can get the name of a witness from a police report, but it hadn't been entered in the Padilla case. I'd already checked. That night I stopped by the shop to see the Kid. His head was buried under the hood of a Chevy truck that had seen a hundred thousand hard miles and was likely to see a hundred thousand more. Trucks live a long and active life in New Mexico. When aged properly, they are as respected and venerated as elders. "How's your search coming?" I asked.

The Kid kept his head buried in the engine. "What search?"

"For the witness."

"I'm working on it."

"Work harder. Work faster. I need to know," I told him.

"Hijole!" he replied in annoyance.

"Hello," squawked his parrot.

A few days later, when he was in the bedroom getting ready for bed, he reached deep into his pocket and came up with a grubby slip of paper that had a name and address hand-printed on it. The name was Alfredo Lobato. The address was on Pino in a neighborhood where gangs hang out.

"How'd you get this?" I asked him.

"Lobato started talking. Someone who knew I was looking heard him and gave it to me."

"It's the weakness of the criminal personality."

"What?"

"Talking. They always have to tell somebody what they've done."

"How do you know the guy is a criminal?"

"You're right, I don't know. If he told the truth about what he saw, he's not a criminal, not in this case anyway." And if he was telling the truth about what he'd seen, my client wasn't a criminal, either. "Saia believes he's not a gang member. Is that true?"

The Kid was not impressed by Saia's street knowledge. "My guy says he's a Four O."

"What does he look like?"

"I never saw him, but *mi amigo* says he is *muy feo*. He has a *barba de chivo*—a little beard like a goat— only his is on the back of his head."

"That should make him easy to identify."

"You're not going to talk to him, are you, chiquita?"

"Why not?"

"These guys are *muy peligroso.*"

"I know."

"Stay away from them." The Kid bent down, kissed my cheek and sniffed my hair. "It smells good now that you are not smoking."

"You can tell the difference?"

"Sure." Now that his pockets were empty, he began unbuttoning his shirt and unbuckling his belt, turned on maybe by the subject of danger and smoke-free hair. He smelled pretty good himself, and I met him naked on the sheets.

The next morning I went to work by way of Rosa Street, driving across the railroad tracks, past the Sacred Heart soccer field and church, the adobes with historical markers, the warehouses, the strip joints and into the neighborhood where Alfredo Lobato lived. Somewhere in there I crossed the city/county line. On Rosa you can go from rural charm to city trash in one long block.

After I crossed the line I opened the glove compartment, took out the Marlboros I'd been hiding from everyone but myself and lit up. It was a neat trick of Sonia's, blowing out a match with a cigarette in her mouth, and one I'd never been able to perform driving or sitting still. I used my car lighter and put it back in its circular compartment. How many cigarettes a day could I smoke in my car? I asked myself every time I did this, and I'd been doing it more often since I'd begun representing Cheyanne Moran. Not enough to do any harm, my self answered. It beat smoking in the office and at home anyway. Anna and the Kid had never told me to stop—getting caught in a forest fire told me that—but I knew what they'd say if I restarted. Car smoking was my way of keeping it secret. When I was growing up people kept what they did in cars secret. Remembering the Kid's comments about smoke in my hair, I rolled the windows down, allowing the wind to blow in and the smoke to blow out.

When I got to Lobato's street, Pino, I turned down it, wondering why Saia believed he wasn't a gang member when the Kid's informant had said he was and the neighborhood had gang written all over it. Now that I knew where Lobato lived, I felt the same negative pull to his house that I felt to my pack of Marlboros. I wanted to see where he lived and what he looked like. I wanted to judge for myself the quality of Saia's witness. Lobato hadn't been at the arraignment. If anyone there had had a beard on the back of his head, I'd have remembered.

Since I'd never seen Lobato, I figured he wouldn't know who I was, either. Still, I couldn't drive down the street too often without somebody noticing the *huera* in the yellow Nissan. Pino wasn't a road that led anywhere. It was a street of broken cars and houses fortified by burglar bars. The houses were small and close together. The yards were a warren subdivided into tiny cages by chain-link and wooden fences. I didn't see a single person as I drove down Pino, but I had the feeling that curtains were opening and closing behind me. At number 347, the Lobato residence, the blinds were drawn, the driveway was empty. There was a chain-link fence around the bare yard, and attached to the garage was a hoop without a net.

16

Disproving Cade's alibi
had reopened the Padilla case for Saia, and for me it
had reopened the issue of who had assaulted my
client. The police hadn't been very interested in the
assault after Cheyanne had refused to cooperate in
their investigation and had pled guilty to Juan
Padilla's murder. I'd always been more concerned
about that crime than Saia was. It had been and still
was a sticking point for me. Maybe the wounds had
been inflicted by Cade seeking insurance in case his
alibi was disproven, although I wasn't as convinced
as Saia was that the lack of an alibi made Cade guilty.
Still, if he was guilty, Cheyanne could walk. One way

to get to that point was to rule out other possibilities. Maybe the wounds had been self-inflicted in remorse or (as Saia had said) to get into the D Home. If the word on the street had convicted my client of Juan's murder, the assault could have been a payback from the Four O's. I also couldn't exclude the ex-con, gang member and stepfather of sorts, Leo Ortega. He had the muscles, he'd had the opportunity, he had the anger.

On Saturday the Kid worked and I had nothing special to do, so in the afternoon I took a walk to the Sacred Heart Church to see if there was a soccer game going on. About halfway down the block I saw a mix of Mercedes-Benzes, Toyotas, four-by-fours and pickup trucks lined up on both sides of the street, soccer moms and dads being Saturday chauffeurs. The bike rack was full. The spectators were a fence surrounding the field. Through the spaces between them I could see boys Danny Ortega's age galloping up and down, full of energy, but not very coordinated. I circled around the spectators looking for Leo. Some parents were busy watching the game. Some were busy watching each other. When I located Leo on the far side of the field it was obvious he was in the game-watching category. Whatever the other parents were doing or saying or wearing or driving didn't interest him. He didn't even notice me sidling up beside him. I followed the direction of his

eyes and saw Danny run down the field, take a wild
kick at a ball, lose his balance and fall on his butt.

"Ouch," I said.

"Hey." Leo looked over at me.

"How's Danny's team doing?"

He laughed. "Losing again, but he sure does love
to play. How's Cheyanne?"

"She seems to be all right."

"That's good."

Leo's eyes returned to the field, where Danny
had picked himself up and started running again.
There was a paper cup in Leo's left hand and he
raised his arm to take a sip. The Virgin of Guadalupe
slipped out from under the sleeve of his t-shirt and
embedded in his right forearm I could see the other
tattoo. What I had seen earlier as a chain I now saw
as four zeros.

"What gang were you a member of?" I asked him.

"Why do you want to know?" he replied.

"Was it the Four O's?"

He looked at his arm, saw that the tattoo was
plainly visible and owned up.

"How'd you get out?"

"I didn't. Gangs are like family. You never get
out, but you can get away and that's what I did. I just
don't have anything to do with them. They're more
interested in ranking in the young ones anyway than
they are in me."

"How do they feel about your girlfriend's daughter pleading guilty to Juan Padilla's murder?"

"I haven't discussed it with them."

"There couldn't be many Four O's your age left." I doubted if Leo was thirty-five, but he'd probably lived long enough to be an elder statesman in gangland.

"Not outside the pen," he said.

"If they consider you family, I suppose there is a lot of pressure to rank Danny in."

"Too much," he said. He turned toward me and his eyes blazed with a fire I hadn't seen even when he'd been sniping at Cheyanne. No one is as fierce as the converted—or those who want you to believe they're converted. "But they're not gettin' him. My son's not dying when he's fifteen. My son's not gonna be in the State Pen. My son's gonna grow up and get a job and take care of me when I'm an old man."

The game ended, and Danny galloped over to us. Leo pulled him close and ruffled his hair, which—today anyway—happened to be grease-free. Some children seem to be born good. Some children get told it so often they start to believe it. Hard to tell which of those categories Danny fit into, but he was a good kid. I wondered whether that was a quality that was fixed for life or if there was still time for the gang predators to get ahold of him and turn him into one of them.

A sandy-haired soccer dad approached Leo and they started making plans for next week's game. The other dad wore khakis and a polo shirt. His eyes were a faded blue. Leo dropped his arms to his side, hiding his tattoos.

"This is the best facility in the city," the dad said. "You know that?"

"It's pretty good," Leo replied. "I've been watching your boy. He has a lot of talent."

"You think so?" The dad beamed.

"Sure."

"Danny's coming along well."

"That's good to hear."

While Danny watched his dad with admiring eyes, I wandered off and examined the crowd. A soccer field is one place where the colors of Albuquerque come together, where junker meets Mercedes-Benz and what matters is enthusiasm for the game. Sports have long been a way out of one life and into another. I saw brown, white, Asian and black kids with matching and unmatching parents. The one thing the parents had in common was that they all had plans for their children. The Kid and I wouldn't have stood out here, except that he was closer to the soccer players' age than I was.

Some girls gathered at one end of the field. They could have been cheerleaders, but they'd taken no interest in the game. They were just hanging out, looking at boys, comparing fingernails. I saw Patricia and walked over to say hello. When she spotted me coming she separated from the other girls and met me about ten feet away. Her fingernails were nearly an inch long. Her lips were black. She was wearing a chain around her neck that said BITCH in silver letters. Her pager was attached to the waistband of her skirt.

"How's it going?" I asked her.

"Okay."

"Do you talk to Cheyanne?"

"Every day."

"She's doing better than I expected."

"Oh, sure, she's doin' great in jail twenty-four–seven," Patricia scoffed.

"Twenty-four–seven?"

"All day every day. She's gonna be spending the best years of her life in the Girls' School."

"The judge hasn't accepted her plea yet."

"He will. Did you see the way he looked at her? Even if he doesn't, her life still won't be worth nothin'. She's only thirteen and already her life is over."

"It's not over. Life does get better when you get older."

"But you don't have any fun."

"I don't know. My boyfriend and I have some good times."

"He's still young!" she said.

"Not that young," I replied.

"Cheyanne'll die if she goes to the Girls' School. She can't spend two years in that place." Spoken with the intense conviction of a fourteen-year-old. It was like witnessing an oath, as if Patricia had slashed her finger and mixed her blood with Cheyanne's for all time.

If Cheyanne did get two years and got out before her time was up, it wouldn't be the first (or last) time someone escaped from the D Home or the Girls' School. The escapees usually got caught, but not always. "If you're thinking escape, don't even consider it," I said.

"Two years is forever!"

"No, it's not. It'll be over before you know it." I had enough mileage on me by now to put two years in perspective. "Your friend Nolo Serrano talked to me after the arraignment."

"Him? He's not my friend."

"He said he'd look out for Cheyanne while she's inside."

"The only person Nolo looks out for is himself." Patricia glanced at her sports watch. "I gotta go."

"Where?"

"Home."

"I'm going downtown to my office. I can give you a ride."

I could see her mentally comparing me to the bus and deciding I was better, but not by much. "Okay," she said. "As soon as I turn fifteen my parents are giving me a car. No more rides. No more bus."

"Cool," I said.

The soccer crowd was breaking up and heading for their cars, trucks and bikes. Patricia and I walked down Mirador toward my house. While we waited for the long light at Second she turned around and saw that Danny had left his father behind at the soccer field and was following us on his bike. "Hey, bro," she called. Danny waved.

"He follows me a lot now," Patricia said.

"How come?"

"He doesn't have his sister to follow anymore."

"She didn't like it much."

"It doesn't bother me. I don't have a little brother."

"Do you have any brothers or sisters?"

"Only Cheyanne. She's like my sister."

The light changed and we crossed Second. It's hard to make small talk with a teenager. Besides, the things I wanted to talk about were not small, so I went ahead and asked her what I wanted to know. Either she'd answer or she wouldn't. If I'd been Detective Jessup I'd have tried flattery, but that's not my style.

"I could have done more for Cheyanne if she'd

told me who or what got her out of the house the night she was assaulted," I said. "If she'll say it was Ron Cade, I may be able to get her out of the D Home."

Patricia said nothing, and we kept on walking. We reached my house and stood outside in front of the courtyard.

"She doesn't like Leo much, does she?" I tried again.

That got a response. "She hates him. They're always duking it out."

"Why?"

"He thinks he's the head honcho. He tries to tell her what to do. He's not her father."

I'd been focused on our conversation and hadn't noticed how close Danny had come. He had a way of turning into a shadow when he rode his bike. Whether he was within earshot or not I couldn't tell.

"Did they fight that night?" I said, lowering my voice as if Patricia and I were conspirators, but that could only happen if she confided in me. She closed her eyes and considered it for a minute, but when she opened them again I could see I was one of those people over thirty she couldn't trust.

"I can't tell you what happened that night."

"You have to trust somebody." She was a savvy fourteen-year-old but way young to be dealing with matters of life and death by herself. She'd erected a wall, however, and I didn't know the way in.

Her eyes were opaque. "I trust Cheyanne. She trusts me." She looked at her watch again. "I gotta go."

"Okay." I walked down the driveway to get the car, and when I came back Danny had pedaled home.

Patricia directed me to her house, which was several blocks south of Mirador on one of the streets that still resembles a country road. She lived in a frame stucco dwelling in the middle of a large lot surrounded by a chain-link fence. It wasn't much of a place, but I figured Patricia's bedroom would be pink and plush and full of gadgets like the computer she knew how to operate and the pager she always wore. The west side of the property bordered the Chapuzar Lateral, the ditch that crossed Mirador near my house and the Morans' trailer. It was a cool and shady walk from her place to mine in the daytime, but at night the predators roamed and La Llorona would be out weeping and looking for her lost children. On the ditch side of the field the fence was topped by circles of wire.

Two orange chows had dug holes in the dirt next to the fence, and they leapt up when I parked. One growled, the other stood still and watched. As soon as Patricia stepped out the door they ran toward her wagging their tails.

"Hi, guys," she said.

She pulled a key ring from her purse and began unlocking the padlock that held the gate shut. Someone was going to a lot of effort to keep this place and/or Patricia safe. Maybe it was living in a fortress or maybe it was being an only child that enabled her to be so bold. Cheyanne had the raggedy air of a street dog—sometimes confident and sometimes not—but Patricia seemed better-groomed to me, more pampered, and more reckless as well. "Do your parents own this property?" I asked.

"Yeah."

"I bet they get offers all the time." A couple of acres this close to town would get developers salivating even if the rest of the street was full of yard cars and trailers.

"All the time," she said. "But my dad won't sell. He grew up here."

"What does he do?"

"They run a temp business. They work twenty-four–seven."

She let herself in, locked the gate behind her, stopped to pet the dogs. "Thanks for the ride," she said.

"*De nada,*" I replied.

I hadn't intended go to my office. My intention had been to question Patricia, but all I'd learned was where she lived, that she was an only child, that she had parents who worked all the time, that her home life might be more stable than Cheyanne's but lonelier and that she considered Cheyanne a blood relative. I'd thought about asking her if she knew Alfredo Lobato, but that was a name I felt I ought to be keeping to myself. His name and address and the question of why he'd fingered Ron Cade if Cheyanne had shot Juan Padilla was a sore tooth I couldn't stop touching. After I dropped Patricia off, I lit a cigarette and went out cruising.

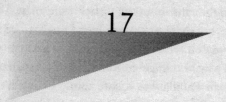

17

I intended my final des-
tination to be Alfredo Lobato's house, but I had a
couple of other names and addresses in my pocket to
check out first. I cut over to Second, went north to
Paseo del Norte and headed east toward the foothills.
Paseo is a limited-access highway until you reach the
Interstate; after that it becomes four lanes, then nar-
rows down to two. I passed the corner where a guy
was selling bears he'd carved with a chainsaw and
someone else was selling red chile ristras. This used to
be an empty part of town, but it was filling up. The
land on my right had been turned into identical brick
houses that had four thousand square feet inside but

only fifteen feet between them. Behind a sign reading RUNNING RIDGE ESTATES, the land on the left was just starting to be developed. I turned into the mostly vacant development of one-acre lots. Each of the few houses was surrounded by several undeveloped acres, an island in the high, barren desert.

I found the address I'd been looking for. The house was brand-new, with no neighbors and no landscaping. It was large and ugly, as if wings from houses of different styles and periods had been slapped together. The doors to the three-car garage faced the street. The house's windows—looking west toward the long view—were as blank as eyes that had been sealed shut by cataracts. This was the place where Ron Cade lived if Ron Cade ever came home.

I took Paseo back to I–25, went south to Lomas, drove to the country club and looked for the second house on my list. This was an old and settled neighborhood with expensive landscaping and big trees. Professional people with money who wanted to be close to downtown lived here. The house I'd been looking for was white stucco with a red-tile roof in the California mission style. The windows had the scrolls and loops of elaborate burglar bars. The message inscribed thereon was "keep out." There was a wall around the property and an intercom at the gate. It took only a half hour to get from Ron Cade's residence to here, but I felt better about Henry

O'Brien Jr.'s safety after I saw the place. Gang members would be noticed in this neighborhood. Henry would be protected if he had the brains to stay home, if his craving for coke allowed him to stay home, if his father made him stay home.

I went east on Lomas and north on Rosa to Alfredo Lobato's hood, where walls spray-painted with graffiti were part of the scenery. It was art or vandalism, depending on your point of view. Recently a cleanup crew hadn't been able to tell the difference and had painted over a commissioned work of art, which hadn't made the artist happy.

I'd never driven by Lobato's place on a Saturday. When I'd yielded to the impulse it had been a weekday. I hadn't seen anybody in the street, and as far as I knew, no one had seen me. I told myself that once I was noticed I'd stop. Cruising Pino on a Saturday when there was bound to be somebody out was a way of pushing the envelope.

The minute I turned the corner I saw a bunch of teenagers taking up a lot of space in their wide clothes. I saw the clothes as a means of intimidation, and it worked for me. I'd thought of putting my thirty-eight in the glove compartment before I left home; people get shot nowadays for wearing the wrong colors or driving into the wrong hood. But I'd seen too many possibilities for disaster and had left the gun at home. On the other hand, leaving it at home might have encouraged disaster of another kind.

One of the girls looked a lot like Laura from the arraignment. When she saw me she put her hand over her mouth and said something to her friends. I didn't see the only other gangbanger I knew—Nolo Serrano. I hadn't put him on my drive-by list because there were too many Serranos in the phone book to narrow my search. As I approached the gang they fanned out until they covered the width of the street. I tried driving onto the shoulder and cutting around them but two guys in "smile now, cry later" shirts stepped in front of me. It was run them down or stop.

"You looking for somebody?" one of the guys asked.

"Is this Calle Llorca?" I asked back.

The gangster's pants went beyond baggy, his smile radiated menace, four O's were tattooed across his right forearm, there was a conspicuous bulge under his t-shirt. Just in case I missed the point, he lifted the shirt to show me the Tech Nine he was packing between his boxer shorts and the waistband of his pants. "You're on the wrong street," he said.

"How do I get to Llorca?" I asked, trying to keep my voice level, showing neither fear nor disrespect. I figured looking into his hostile eyes could be considered a dis, so I focused on his comedy and tragedy masks instead. *You're an adult,* I told myself. *You're a lawyer. He's a punk.* Still, he had the gun and this was his turf. On the other hand, my foot was on the gas pedal and a Nissan could be considered a weapon, too.

Maybe he realized that. Maybe he wasn't in a killing mood. He looked away from me and pointed deeper into the hood. "Go that way. Turn left."

"Okay," I said.

The homeboys stepped aside to let me pass, watched for a minute to make sure I kept on going, then turned around and walked in the direction of Rosa with their *cojones* intact. I could see in my rearview mirror that the back of their t-shirts read RIP and that no one wore a goatee on the back of his head.

I drove slowly toward the end of the block. There were people out today washing their cars, pounding their boom boxes, playing with their kids or standing around talking. Everybody stared at me, but nobody made a move. I craved a cigarette, but didn't want to take my eyes off the street long enough to light one. When I got to number 347 I saw someone in the driveway throwing a basketball at the hoop without a net. He was a big guy with a head shaved bald and shiny except for the hair at the nape of his neck that had been slicked into the shape of a goatee. His mourning shirt read JUAN PADILLA RIP.

Maybe my car had an unfamiliar rattle or the people on Pino had finely tuned antennae. Like everybody else, Lobato stopped and stared when he heard me coming. He picked up his basketball and cradled it in his arm. His eyes were small and close together. His skin was pockmarked. Even by gang standards, he looked mean and ugly.

I peered into my rearview mirror and saw that the black cloud of gangsters had left Pino, so I pulled over. Lobato stared at me. I stared back. His stare was duller than the other kids', as if he wore protective lenses made of tinted glass. I rolled down the window and asked, "Do you know where Rafael Contreras lives?"

"Uh-uh," he said. He turned around, shot his ball at the basket and missed.

I rolled up my window and drove on. I had the right to question Lobato about the Padilla shooting, but this wasn't the time or the place. One objective had been accomplished, anyway—to see what kind of person he was. I hadn't been impressed by the quality of Saia's witness no matter how well he'd stuck to his story. His Four O's t-shirt discredited him in my mind. I didn't consider gang members reliable, especially if they had a score to settle. But Saia had an agenda and that agenda had been Ron Cade. When it came to the truth about Lobato's gang affiliation, maybe Saia had been hearing what he wanted to hear, believing what he wanted to believe. When I reached the end of the block I did as I'd been told and turned left, wondering why Alfredo Lobato was home alone and not out cruising with the rest of the gang.

I turned onto Llorca and headed back toward Rosa looking at more of the same: graffiti walls, children playing, guys washing their cars, women talking, most of them paying far less attention to my passing than the people on Pino had. That street had pulsated with paranoia. I stopped at Rosa, waiting for the traffic to clear and watching a woman step off her porch, walk across the corner lot and unlatch a chain-link gate. When she reached the street she waved. There was nobody in a hurry behind me, so I waited to see what she wanted. She wore bedroom slippers and a black dress. Her white hair tumbled out of her bun. Her legs were as thick as tree trunks. Her face was furrowed. Her eyes were dark. When she reached the Nissan I rolled down my window.

"Could you give me a ride to the Seven-Eleven?" she asked.

"Okay," I said.

She shuffled around to the passenger side, and I unlocked the door to let her in. She lowered herself slowly to the seat and locked the door behind her. "Do you play Powerball?" she asked me.

"No."

"I won two hundred dollars last week. Why don't you play?"

"I don't like to gamble. Life is risky enough."

"That's true," she admitted. "Life is very risky." She didn't say anything else until I'd driven the five blocks north to the 7-Eleven. Driving on Rosa was a gamble, too, and we both gave it our full attention. Her foot tapped an imaginary brake whenever she thought I wasn't reacting fast enough. I reached the 7-Eleven and parked without being sideswiped or rear-ended or provoked into giving anybody the finger. My passenger put her hand on the door handle and asked, "Will you wait while I buy my ticket?"

"Sure," I said.

I had parked behind a Dumpster with a sign on it that read FOR STORE USE ONLY. I watched a guy drive up, dump a large bag of his own trash and speed off. In a few minutes my passenger was back with a scratch ticket and a quart of milk. She sat down, patiently scraped the black goo off her ticket, sighed and said, "Not this time."

"Do you want me to take you home?"

"Yes, but leave me on Rosa, please. It's not good for you to be seen in my neighborhood. I remember you from the courtroom. Do you remember me?"

"Yes."

"Maybe somebody else will remember you, too."

"You were related to Juan?"

"I am his grandmother."

"You're a Padilla?"

She nodded. "I have thirty-five grandchildren. Do you believe that? He is the third one to die. It's not right when the grandchildren die before the grandmother."

I couldn't disagree with that.

"Why were you on Llorca?" she asked me.

"I was looking for someone."

"On my street?"

"No. On Pino."

"There are a lot of gang members on Pino. Which one were you looking for?"

I looked into Grandmother Padilla's eyes and saw a well in which my information could settle to the bottom and sink into the sediment. Still, I wasn't eager to give up the name of a witness. It could be risky for me, it could be risky for the witness.

"Was it Alfredo Lobato?" she asked.

"Why do you think that?"

"He told everybody he saw the murder and that the killer was the white boy."

"Ron Cade."

"If he saw Ron Cade, why did you let that pretty little girl say she did it?"

"Ron Cade had an alibi. My client didn't. She knew things about the crime that the police didn't reveal. She was spotted near the crime scene around the time of the murder."

"Was she afraid?"

"Very."

"In my time boys killed each other. Girls didn't do things like that. And now they are murderers, too?"

"Sometimes."

"Alfredo is a sad boy." She tapped the side of her head with her forefinger. "Mean, but not very smart."

"Are you related to him, too?"

"Not that I know of." Her brown eyes twinkled, and I saw the spirit of a young and lively woman. "For a long time nobody wanted Alfredo. He was a want-to-be. Even the gang didn't want him, but then I see him wearing the shirt. I think you will want to know why he was accepted, but I don't think you should come looking here again."

I'd reached the corner of Llorca and parked on the far side of Rosa.

"I can walk from here," she said. "Thank you very much for the ride."

"Thank you for the advice." I handed her my card. "Call me if you think of anything else."

She stared at my name and address, fingered the card and put it in her pocket. "I have one more word of advice for you," she said.

"What's that?"

"Play Powerball."

"I'll remember that."

She let herself out of the car. I waited for the light to change and the traffic to clear, then watched her walk across the street holding the milk carton in her hand.

That night over Tecate, tequila and a couple of burritos from Arriba Tacos, I told the Kid I'd seen Alfredo Lobato, but I didn't tell him I'd also seen a gun.

"What'd Lobato look like?" the Kid asked.

"Big, ugly. Like you said, he has a goatee on the back of his head."

"Where did you see him?"

"I drove by his house on Pino. He was outside shooting baskets. I stopped and asked for directions. You were right about his being a member of the Four O's; he was wearing a Juan Padilla mourning shirt."

"That DA guy was wrong."

"Maybe not. Maybe Lobato became a witness first and a Four O later."

"I told you to stay away from those guys. You never know when to stop, chiquita."

And how many times had I heard that one? Sometimes the tightrope I walked on had no net, which was one reason the Kid liked me whether he'd admit it or not. If I didn't go looking for excitement, he'd be *aburrido como una ostra*, bored as an oyster. "Why should I stop?"

"Because it's dangerous."

I shrugged and took a sip of my tequila.

"You never listen to me," he complained.

"You never say anything new," I replied, wondering how much time it took with someone before you began repeating yourself. He had nothing to say to that, and we finished the burritos in silence. While I cleaned up he watched *Walker, Texas Ranger*, his favorite bad and violent TV show. Some people watch violence so they don't have to do it; some people watch it and get inspired to do it. When the Kid is angry he becomes silent, not violent. He was still fuming when we went to bed, which meant he wasn't talking. He can go to bed angry and fall sound asleep and I can't. I lay awake watching him toss and turn and thinking about how complicated men are. At least women can talk about what's bothering them and get rid of it. Problems (especially men problems) are a hot potato that women toss from hand to hand. But men don't talk at all or they talk about cars and sports while the wheels inside keep turning and churning. *Compared to the Kid I'm simple,* I thought. *Basically I have two moods. Either I'm pissed off or I'm not.*

18

The Kid spent Sunday
afternoon lying on the sofa watching a baseball game
and keeping to his vow of silence. I spent the afternoon working in the front yard waiting to see if
Danny would pedal by. My front yard is surrounded
by a low wooden fence. The enclosure is about the
size of a bathroom, but I found enough to do. There
were Siberian elm shoots everywhere. I gave them a
tug, but they didn't want to come out of the holes
they'd burrowed in the ground, so I took a pair of
clippers and snipped them off at the root. When I
had a pile I carried it down the driveway and
dumped it behind the garage.

I continued my weed therapy by stepping outside my yard and working the area in front of the fence, which gave me a clear view of the trailer. Leo's truck and Sonia's Thoroughbred Toyota were parked out front. If anyone came out I'd see them and they'd see me, but nobody did. The shoulder of Mirador Road was where the tough weeds grew. They were about eighteen inches tall, with sage green leaves and a delicate lavender flower, but were hard and thorny as a homegirl. I yanked at them and got bloody fingers and a palm full of prickers. I went back to the garage, found an old pair of gloves and continued tugging. Weeding isn't fun, but at least you can see that you've accomplished something. The ice-cream truck drove by tinkling lullaby and good night, but it didn't pull anybody out of their homes.

The pricker pile was building and I was getting hot and sweaty when the Kid pushed open the door to take a commercial, pee and/or silence break.

"You're gardening, chiquita?" he said.

"So?"

"I never saw you do that before."

"Isn't there a baseball game on?"

"Sure," he said, shutting the door.

I returned to my tugging. My gray nemesis climbed up the courtyard wall and studied me as if it might pounce. I threw a handful of weeds in its direction and it leapt down only to reappear on the far side of the courtyard still watching, but beyond the reach of my throwing arm. All my bad dreams and dark thoughts seemed to have coalesced into the form of a street cat hungry for my catnip patch. The pacing and watching could be seen as my punishment for giving in and feeding its addiction. I know it's better to face your demons than it is to sublimate them, but I was getting sick of this one. "You don't have to supply every junkie on the block," I told myself. "You could get rid of this cat by yanking the catnip out." I was thinking about doing it when I heard the squeal of Danny's bike. The cat heard it, too, and raced down the driveway.

I straightened up and let go of the weed I'd been tugging. The best thing about gardening is how good it feels to stop. I put my hand against my back and stretched a kink out. Danny was approaching from an unexpected direction—the ditch instead of the trailer—and looking hot and sweaty himself.

He pedaled up beside me, dropped his kickstand to the ground and watched the cat as it disappeared behind the house. "That cat gives me a hinky feeling," he said. "Like Goosebumps."

"I don't like it, either," I replied.

"What are you doing?" he asked.

"Weeding."

"Can I help?"

"I'm done. How about a glass of water or lemonade?"

"Lemonade," he said.

I went into the house, came back with two lemonades and we sat down on the *banco* in the courtyard to drink them.

"Patricia told me you've been following her on your bike," I began.

"Sometimes I do," he said.

"Are you worried about her?"

He nodded. "Look what happened to my sister."

"You're nine years old, Danny." The dangerous age, when a boy would do anything to be accepted. "You should leave this stuff to the grown-ups." He gave me a look that implied he didn't think the grown-ups had been doing so hot so far. "You miss your sister, don't you?"

"A lot." He swung his heels and kicked the *banco*. "She could be mean, but she didn't let anybody punk me."

"Somebody tried to punk you?"

"The gangs thought I was a Four O because my dad used to be, but I'm not."

"Your dad tries real hard to keep you out of the gangs, doesn't he?"

"Yeah, but he doesn't live here and Cheyanne did."

"She and your dad fought?"

He nodded. "All the time."

"Did they fight the night she got beat up?"

"No." Today his hair was grease-free and it fell into loose and floppy bangs. He brushed them away from his face. "She was in her room. Him and me, we were watching TV."

"What was it that got Cheyanne out of the house? Do you know?"

"I think somebody beeped her and she climbed out the window."

"Cheyanne had a beeper?"

He finished his lemonade and put the glass down on the *banco*. "It was an old one of Patricia's. She said it was big and ugly and it didn't even vibrate. She didn't want it no more."

"What happened to the beeper after Cheyanne went to the D Home?" I asked.

"I have it."

"Did you tell the police?"

"No."

"Did you show it to your mom or dad?"

"Cheyanne said not to. She said they'd go off if they knew. I locked in the last message she got."

"Could I see it?"

He saw that I wasn't about to go off and said, "Okay."

He biked down the road and in a few minutes came back with the beeper hidden under his shirt. We took it into the courtyard and shut the door behind us. The beeper looked like a guy's model,

plain and black with a belt clip on the side. I could
see why Patricia wanted a new one. Since I was
beeper-illiterate, I asked Danny to show me how it
worked.

"When somebody calls you, see, their message or
their number shows up here." He pointed to the tiny
LCD screen, which happened to be blank at the
moment. "Some beepers have letters, but those ones
cost a lot. Kids don't have that kind, so they use the
numbers for letters. This beeper only has numbers.
You can leave a code if you want to so people will
know it's you."

"A code?"

"That's like a tag," he said.

I stared at the blank little screen, but it told me
nothing. Danny pushed the lock-in button. A little
padlock appeared in the corner and the number
6656 showed up. "That's the code of the person who
called Cheyanne," he said.

"What does it mean?"

"I don't know."

"Do you know who it is?"

"No."

"Do those numbers represent letters?"

"5 is S, but 6 isn't anything."

"Could it be a B?"

"No. That's 8."

He pushed another button and what looked like

a phone number came up. "I think that's a beeper number," he said.

"How can you tell?"

"Because the beeper company that everybody goes to uses those first three numbers."

He pushed the button again and the sequence 01*10*17335 appeared. "That means see you at the ditch at ten."

"Huh?"

He flipped the pager over and showed me the numbers reversed and upside down. "5 is S, 3 is E, 17 is U. That's see you. 01 is a D or an A. But this time I think it's a D and it means ditch. Star is at. And 10 is 10."

"Oh," I said.

"There are a lot of messages that kids send. 177 0 177 or 303, that's MOM. 304 upside down, that means hoe."

"As in whore?"

"Right. 304*55318008, do you know what that means?"

"I can't imagine."

"Do you have any of those yellow stick-on things?"

"Post-its?"

"Yeah."

I went inside and got him a pad of Post-its and a pen. He wrote the message down for me, but I couldn't decipher it.

"Look at it upside down."

I still couldn't imagine what it meant.

"Boobless hoe," he said.

The creative imagination of kids boggled the mind. The game was time-consuming and seductive. Already I was wondering if the word boggle could translate into numbers.

17*31707*1, Danny wrote. "That's I love you."

"I'll remember that," I said. "Are there any other messages stored?"

"No. With this beeper you can only lock in one."

"Did you call the number?" I asked him.

Danny nodded. "I called one time when I was at my dad's for the weekend. I left his number but nobody called back. Some people don't answer even when they get your message. They say they forgot their beeper or their battery went dead. Or they got a lot of messages and the first ones were erased."

"I think it would be better if you didn't try again."

"Okay," he said. He actually seemed relieved to be finally turning the matter over to an adult.

"Do you want the beeper back?"

"You keep it," he said. "Are you going to call the number?"

"Yes."

"Maybe when you find who that person is you'll find out that my sister didn't kill anybody."

"Maybe so."

"Somebody has to prove she didn't do it," he said with the same fire in his eyes that I'd seen in his dad's.

"I'll do my best," I said.

He got on his bike and rode home without indicating whether he thought my best would be good enough.

I went inside and called Information to see if any of my suspects' beeper numbers were listed and found out that the phone company doesn't list beeper numbers. The police could track the number down if they had just cause, but I couldn't turn it over without my client's consent (which I didn't think would be forthcoming) or involving Danny further, and I didn't want to do that. I dialed the phone number Danny had locked in and got a generic female voice telling me to key in my number at the tone. I thought about leaving a message, but my imagination wasn't up to the job of translating what I had to say into numerical form, so I punched in my office number and hung up. I didn't want to be waiting around my house for some delinquent to show up or call me back. In a way, beepers resembled ditches. They were a current that flowed through the valley. Once you put your number out there you gave someone the power to answer and let the water flow or to shut you off.

I went into the living room, where the baseball game was still on the tube. Nobody happened to be spitting in anybody else's face. The outfielders stood around staring into their gloves and looking bored as oysters. The Kid was sound asleep on the sofa. That's precisely the effect baseball has on me.

I cooked Chile Willies for dinner, and we ate them when the Kid woke up. We watched *Lois and Clark* and a bad movie. I locked up tight before we went to bed. The Kid had reconciliation on his mind, but mine was somewhere else. He rolled over and went to sleep. I lay awake listening for the squeal of a bike, the howl of a cat or the wailing of La Llorona. When I finally fell asleep I dreamed it was the middle of the night and the rattlesnake cat was curled up beside the ditch waiting to eat or get eaten.

19

I got to my office Mon-
day all too aware that my number was out there on the
beeper network. My law office is where I go to be
reminded of how hard people can be. Home is where
I'd like to forget. My home number has been unlisted
since I became a lawyer, and I intended to keep it that
way. My office has burglar bars on the windows and
proximity to downtown law enforcement, and I have
Anna at the door to keep an eye out for riffraff and
punks. On Lead that can keep you occupied 24-7.
When it's quitting time I can lock the door and walk
away. When you own a house you can never walk away.
I told Anna that I'd placed a call that might mean

trouble, to keep the door locked and not let anybody in until I saw who it was and gave my approval.

"I'm okay," she said. "I've got red pepper spray."

"This could be more like semiautomatics than pepper spray," I replied.

"Who'd you call? A postal employee?"

"I don't know who it is. It's a number that was locked in a pager Cheyanne had the night she was beat up."

"Uh-oh," Anna said. "Gangbangers."

"I wouldn't be surprised."

"Girl or guy?"

"I don't know."

"Guy, I hope. I can handle them, but those *cholas* are tough." Anna had certain *chola* attributes herself—tons of hair, a don't-mess-with-me attitude, long fingernails and a high fear threshold. "Do you know what the girls have to do to rank in?"

"Screw?"

"Fight. The girls that are in already beat up the wannabe."

"What kind of weapons do they use?"

"Their hands and their feet. They kick. They punch."

"I couldn't do it," I said. I didn't have any trouble punching guys out, but for me hitting a woman was taboo.

"It wouldn't bother me," Anna said.

"That's because you have sisters."

"We were always fighting. My sister Maria was in a gang. She and her friends liked to play the guys against each other and get them to fight."

"What happened to your sister?"

"She had a baby and moved to Las Cruces."

"Be careful," I said, going into my office.

"No problem," Anna replied, taking her red pepper spray out of her purse and laying it on her desk.

Trying to get some work done was like waiting for water to boil with the burner on low. Waiting for the phone to ring is a feeling every woman knows all too well. You used to be able to relieve the anxiety by performing the stupid woman's trick of calling the guy, then hanging up when he answered. But now your number could appear on a screen and give away your obsession. Caller ID could change mating rituals forever.

The phone at the Hamel Law Office rang several times on Monday. One hang-up, one wrong number. Someone wanting to buy a house. Someone else hoping to get a divorce. A man trying to sell me a credit card. A woman selling long-lasting light bulbs for the handicapped, bulbs that could outlive me.

Ignoring my advice, Anna opened the door for the mailman, a messenger, a guy with a shopping cart who was looking for a handout and her friend

Anita. I was beginning to think that whoever I'd called had let the batteries run down or was not interested in talking to a lawyer. Around five Anna buzzed and said there was a good-looking guy at the door.

"Yours or mine?" I asked. It was the time of day when the Kid and her current boyfriend were liable to show up.

"Neither," she said.

"I'll be right out," I replied.

But by the time I got there Anna had let the guy in. He had pale eyes and delicate features. He wore a black baseball hat turned backward, a black t-shirt and jeans that were only semi-baggy. As far as I could tell, he wasn't carrying a weapon, and he didn't look gang today, which cut some slack for Anna. Still, if it had been me I wouldn't have opened the door.

"Hey," Nolo Serrano said. "You beeped me."

"That's right," I said.

"I had to be downtown today, so I came over." The expression on his mobile face shifted rapidly from amusement to concern. "Cheyanne's not having trouble in the D Home, is she?"

"Not that I know of."

"How'd you get my pager number?"

"It was on Cheyanne's beeper the night she was assaulted. You asked her to meet you at the ditch at ten."

"Hey." He tapped his beeper and laughed. "You got these things all figured out."

"Did Cheyanne meet you that night?"

"Sure did."

"Why?"

"I wanted to tell her that Ron Cade was looking to jump her."

"Why would he want to do that?"

"I think he was afraid his alibi wasn't gonna hold up. Everybody but the APD knew that Henry O'Brien was a crackhead. I tried to warn Cheyanne about Cade, but she wouldn't believe me. She was crazy about that guy, you know, but man, after what he did to her." He shook his head. "What a buster. She shouldn't be takin' his rap for him. But I'm lookin' out for her, so she'll be all right now." His expression had turned serious, but his eyes still danced. "I hear the alibi didn't hold up."

"Where'd you hear that?" I asked.

"On the street. News gets out." He tapped his beeper. "Those cops should do their job, man, or we're gonna have to do it for 'em."

"Stay out of it," I warned.

"Can't do that. Juan was my homeboy." His beeper gave him a buzz. He looked at the message, which could have been a drug deal, an assignation or a gang command. I didn't think it was from Mom. "Gotta go, man," he said. "Gotta go. You tell Cheyanne everything's cool, not to worry. And you . . . you're lookin' good." He smiled at Anna.

Anna laughed. "I bet the girls are crazy about him," she said when Nolo had danced out the doorway. "He's pretty cute."

"The cuter they are the more trouble they are." It's a lesson women are always willing to forget. "He's a gangbanger."

"He wasn't wearing the clothes."

"Maybe because he came downtown on business."

"Is he really looking out for Cheyanne?"

"He says he is."

"Nothing's happened to her yet, has it?"

"No."

"Could be he has a heart. Not everybody in a gang is a monster."

It was the kind of thing some guys could make you want to believe.

Anna looked at her watch. "Quitting time," she said, putting her red pepper spray back in her purse. "See you *mañana*."

Shortly after she left, I locked up and went home myself. The office had the locks and burglar bars to keep it safe; besides, we had nothing to steal.

The Kid went to bed early. I stayed up watching late-night comedy and chasing the questions that buzzed around my head like flies drawn to a light bulb. Had either of the girls I knew been dumb enough to have fallen for Ron Cade or Nolo Serrano? That Cheyanne loved or feared Cade were premises I'd heard before. All I'd seen from Patricia was contempt for both of them. I didn't suspect either girl of falling for Alfredo Lobato, but he was a key player now that Ron Cade's alibi had disintegrated. Still, a phony alibi didn't prove Cade had pulled the trigger. He could have concocted a story because he'd been involved in some other crime or just to get the police and the Four O's off his back. Ron Cade might have beeped my client the night she was assaulted, but the number Danny locked in had been Nolo Serrano's.

I needed a cigarette, so I got dressed, went out to the car and lit up. Since I was already in my vehicle, it was only a flick of the wrist to turn on the ignition and set it in motion. I contemplated a drive across the Sandia Pueblo, but the Nissan had a mind of its own. It was drawn to Pino like a magnet to a refrigerator. Ignoring Grandmother Padilla's and the Kid's advice, I let it pull me down Rosa and onto Lobato's street. It was late and the streets were empty. The lights were on at 347, the blinds closed and a *muy suave*, red and white, Fast Five Chevy convertible was parked in the driveway. It was a candyman's car, clean, sparkling, polished. Except for the omnipresent thump of a backbeat, the street was quiet. Everybody was either drinking, drugging or sleeping. I didn't linger; I'd seen what I wanted to see. Maybe even what I'd expected to see.

On the way home I smoked another cigarette thinking about what had turned a wannabe into a homeboy. I parked the car in the garage, shut the door, then stood outside and let the wind blow the smoke from my hair. One thing you can count on in Albuquerque is the wind. I crawled into bed, curled up behind the Kid and fell asleep.

A few hours later the sun beaming through the sky-light woke me up. In the morning the red and white Chevy that had seemed so significant the night before seemed more like a mirage or a dream. It proved that Nolo and Alfredo knew each other, but that was to be expected; they belonged to the same gang.

The Kid was sitting at the kitchen table drinking coffee. "Did you go out last night?" he asked me.

"How'd you know that?"

"I woke up. You weren't there. Your car was gone."

"I went by Lobato's house again. A red and white Fast Five Chevy was parked outside."

"A convertible? *Muy suave?*"

"Yup."

"Nolo Serrano's."

"I figured."

"You should stay away from those guys, chiquita. They think nothing of taking your breath away."

"Excuse me?" I'd been reaching for the Mr. Coffee but put my empty cup down on the counter. "What did you say?"

"Take your breath away. That's what they say when they are going to kill somebody."

"I was afraid of that."

"Did somebody say that to you?"

"No. That's what Patricia said in court to Nolo Serrano. I thought she was flirting."

"Does she know what it means?"

"Probably."

"You think she would try to kill him?"

"I hope not."

"Why would she want to?"

"Maybe because he's the one who put her best friend in jail." It could explain what connected the *muy feo* and the *muy suave*. "And those girls have sworn a blood oath to look out for each other."

"What are you going to do about it?"

"Talk to her." It was the only weapon I had, but I doubted it would be good enough.

20

That afternoon I left work early and drove down Candelaria to Valley High School, home of the Vikings. How the Vikings had left their name in the Rio Grande valley was a mystery to me, unless they'd sailed their ships up the river as some people believe the Phoenicians had done. Sitting in my car waiting for school to let out I could have been a parent, I could have been a PI, I could have been a pervert. My quarry might see me as an annoyance or a threat, but I preferred to think of myself as a person seeking the truth. There was a lot of activity outside Valley High, a lot of kids driving away in cars that were newer and more *suave* than mine. While I waited the boys' track team came out of the gym and ran across the parking lot. When they reached the street they dropped their shorts in unison and mooned the lot, showing a bunch of tight white cheeks.

The kids who kept their clothes on were a more frightening prospect. Pleasing was out, ugly was in. I had to keep reminding myself that I'd been a member of the original freak generation. These kids seemed scarier to me, but that could be a matter of age and perspective. The baggy clothes, the shaved heads, the body piercing gave me a hinky feeling. I couldn't help wondering what it would be like to have one of them living in the house. Down the street was close enough for me. The colors they wore were subdued, since wearing the wrong color to school these days could get you killed. Eventually Patricia came out the door surrounded by a gaggle of girl-friends. Patricia was never subdued. She wore a tight teal dress with a matching beeper and was too busy talking to her friends to notice me.

The girls got into a convertible and drove down Candelaria putting air in their hair. I followed them across town to the mall. They parked, went in through the food court entrance and disappeared into the crowd, which was full of teens at this time of day. I circled the food stalls past Panda Express, Burger King, Cajun Fried Food. I figured it would be a while before the girls covered the mall and came back out, so I went to the ladies' room. Peeing can be a problem when you're conducting surveillance. I got myself an iced tea, sat down at one of the little tables and listened to a woman at the next table talking about her cat that existed in a parallel universe.

I knew what the girls would be doing—checking out the guys, throwing sign if they were gang members, saying you mess with one of us you mess with all of us. Where I grew up we used to drive around the town square after high school. Maybe the mall was a better alternative. Less chance for road rage and it saved on gas. It was two hours before the girls came back out. By then I was bored as an oyster. I was hidden behind a potted plant, so Patricia didn't see me when she walked by.

The girls got into their car, and I followed them back across town to Charlie's Drive-In on Fourth, which was known for its chile fries. There was no way to hide my car at Charlie's, so I parked at the strip mall across the street. Surveillance consists of hours of deep boredom punctuated by bursts of minor excitement. Eventually the girls left Charlie's and drove north. By the time her friends let Patricia off at her house it was eight o'clock, but no one seemed to be home. The outside sensor lights had come on, spreading long shadows across the scraped-bare yard. The interior of the house was dark and no cars were parked out front. The dogs greeted Patricia by jumping against the fence and rattling the chain links. When I pulled up beside her Patricia gave me a hard stare. I rolled down the window.

"We need to talk," I said.

"About what?"

"Nolo Serrano."

"What about him?"

"I saw him yesterday. He told me he beeped Cheyanne the night she was assaulted and that's what got her out of the house. He said he warned her to look out for Ron Cade."

Patricia flipped a curl across her shoulder. "That's his story." Patricia was a pretty girl, a girl whose phone would always be ringing, whose beeper would always be beeping, whose mailbox would always be full. I hoped she'd be smart enough to choose the right invitations to answer.

"Why did you tell Nolo at the arraignment that you'd take his breath away?" I asked her.

"I said that?"

"Yeah. I heard you, but I didn't find out until this morning what it meant."

"I was talking smack. It didn't mean nothin'."

"Stay away from Nolo, Patricia. He's dangerous."

"Not as dangerous as he thinks he is."

"Do you want me to call the police?"

She laughed. "Oh, yeah, they're really gonna do something."

"They might." I could give the APD what I had, the beeper message, but with no date it was useless as evidence. And there was still the problem of my client's cooperation. I couldn't spring her if she didn't want to be sprung. But there are times when private citizens have means of solving crimes the police don't.

"I'm not counting on the police," Patricia said.

"Stay out of it," I warned her.

"Sure," she replied. She unlocked the padlock, let herself in and walked across the yard to the empty house. At least she had the dogs and her pager for company.

I hadn't gotten very far with Patricia, and I didn't expect to get anywhere with my client either, but the next day I went to see her in the D Home. It still surprised me that two girls so young could be so stubborn. Usually the will hardens at about the same rate as the arteries. I'd seen fear in Cheyanne, which might be her excuse, but I hadn't seen any fear in Patricia. Just a real strong will.

My client was making her blue uniform with the numbers and letters on the back look pretty good. The dullness I'd seen on earlier visits had been replaced by excitement. Her movements were quicker, her eyes were brighter. I suspected she'd already talked to Patricia, but I told her my tale about running into Nolo Serrano anyway. It wasn't the whole truth, but I didn't want to get Danny in trouble, and I didn't want to reveal that I had the piece of the puzzle that was the beeper. Besides, I always had the excuse that I was the adult and the lawyer and that what I was doing was for her own good. She listened carefully, as if she hadn't heard the story before or was listening for some nuance that Patricia had missed.

"Nolo should keep his mouth shut," was her response.

"So who was it that assaulted you? Nolo or Ron Cade? Who were you covering for?"

She squeezed her hands into a wad of fingernails and rings. "I can't say. They'd kill me."

"You *are* in the D Home, Cheyanne."

"It doesn't matter. They can hit you here just as fast as on the street."

"If it was Cade, his alibi's been disproven. Like I told you, with your cooperation the police could arrest him for Juan's murder, and you'd be out of here." If it had been Nolo it would be more problematical.

"I know you're trying to help, but don't. I'm cool here, and it ain't gonna be forever."

They didn't allow beepers in the D Home, but these girls could do a lot with a phone—too much. "If you and Patricia are planning something, stop. These guys are violent and ruthless."

"Have you seen Danny boy?" she asked me, changing the subject.

"Yeah. He told me he misses you."

"He's a dork, but he's my bro. It sets me off that I can't do nothin' for him in here."

"What could you do for him out there?"

"Keep them Four O's off his back."

When I got home I took out Patricia's discarded black beeper that had ended up in Cheyanne's hands. I held it in my palm, where it was a neat fit, and pushed the on switch. The beeper responded by squealing a few times; then a bunch of bubbles appeared on the LCD screen. I pushed the message button. There were a lot of them–codes and numbers that meant something to someone but not much to me. It occurred to me that this was a satellite beeper still connected to Patricia's number, and that she hadn't disconnected it when she got the new one. Patricia could have read the messages Cheyanne received and I could read the messages she received— if I could decipher them.

I pressed the button that recalled the message

from Nolo Serrano that Danny had locked in. It was still there on this beeper, although it probably wouldn't be locked in on the newer model. I figured the beepers received communally but stored individually. I began clicking through Patricia's messages. I didn't see Nolo Serrano's number, which was the only one I'd recognize. Most of the numbers had the first three digits of the popular beeper company. One message I saw several times was 304*14, hi hoe. I saw a few MOM's and a lot of 17*31707*1, I love you's. The code for that particular message was 77. I wondered what that meant. Initials? The year of a car? A birthdate? If so, that guy was too old to be saying I love you to Patricia.

I began checking her messages a couple of times a day. I got a queasy feeling every time the bubbles rose to the surface of the LCD screen, but the messages I could decipher tended to be teen trivia—a lot of hi's, a lot of hoe's, a lot of I love you's. I wouldn't have minded hearing that one as much as Patricia did.

I called Saia and asked him if he'd located Ron Cade.

"Still working on it," he said. "He's one slippery son of a bitch."

"I think there's trouble brewing in gangland," I told him.

"There's always trouble brewing in gangland. You got anything definite?"

"Not really."

"Give me a call back when you do."

"What's your beeper number?"

"You've joined the beeper network?"

"Sort of."

He gave me his number. "Can I beep you?"

"It would be better if you didn't." Any incoming messages for me could also be read by Patricia.

On Saturday I did my evening beeper check and finally saw the one number and code I recognized. I compared it to the message in Lock-In to be sure. The code was 6656 and the number was the number that had drawn Nolo Serrano into my office. The message was a long one: 00*17*301177*17701117*17335. 17335 upside down was "see you," I knew, but the rest of it was a mystery.

I clicked the message button and found one more message—104. HOL or Hd upside down—or "okay" right side up in the lingo radio operators use. The first three digits told me the callback number was another beeper. I knew from experience that I wouldn't be able to find out who it belonged to from the phone company. The code was 72, but, like 6656, I couldn't decipher what it meant. I'd found 6656 by setting up a meeting in my office, but I doubted there'd be time for that and I didn't want Patricia to know I'd been eavesdropping.

In a way I'd struck gold, but gold that was buried deep in the vein. It seemed that Patricia and Nolo Serrano were planning to meet and that 72 would be joining them. I needed to find out when and where, so I did what I always do when I'm curious—got out my map. If a map doesn't provide answers, it can provide escape. This was a city map showing all the drains, arteries, laterals, ditches, wasteways, streets, lanes, courts, roads, places and trails in town.

I went back to Nolo Serrano's message and tried looking at the second word upside down. Since "see you" had been upside down, it seemed logical that the next word would be, too. I got gobbledygook, but when I flipped the beeper right side up I got 17701117, which could be Main. I'd never heard of a Main Street in Albuquerque; it didn't strike me as a Main Street kind of place. But I checked the street index on my map and found a Main leading out of Old Town. It wasn't a good place for this assignation—too busy, too far away. I figured this meeting would take place closer to Patricia's house, maybe even within walking distance since she wasn't old enough yet for her parents to have bought her a car. My eyes returned to the map and wandered around

the North Valley until they landed on the Main
Canal, which flows from the Sandia Reservation to
the South Valley. This Main could be reached by
starting at the lateral that flowed by Patricia's house
and following the ditch network.

I was getting somewhere, but not near enough,
as the Main Canal was several miles long. I turned
to 301177, the next word. Right side up it was E 0 I
M-E 0 1 M or E d M. I flipped the beeper over. Flipping back and forth was a lot of trouble to go to to
pass on a message, but these words and places could
already be familiar to the participants and they
might not have to go through the gyrations that I
did. Upside down 301177 read Lupe. There were
Lupes all over the Valley. Lupe Road wandered
north and south in the convoluted path of a cow
trail. There was also a Lupe Lane, a Circle, a Court
and a Trail. The Road more or less paralleled the
Main Canal, the Trail crossed it, the Lane, the Circle and the Court came close to abutting it.

I wondered what kind of place these kids would
choose to meet in, protected or secluded. If Patricia
met Nolo Serrano at all, it ought to be in a wide-
open lot with bright lights adjacent to a police station, but there weren't any places like that on the
Main Canal. I turned next to the number 17, which
followed the star sign and meant nothing to me. If it
was the time, it was already past five o'clock, the sev-

enteenth hour. Upside down 17 was a U or a V. I went back to my map and found three places where the Main Canal forked and formed a V near Lupe Circle, Lupe Court and Lupe Lane. They were each about a mile apart.

The next number was 11, somebody's age or—more likely—the time of the scheduled assignation. I looked at the clock—nine-thirty, which gave me only an hour and a half.

I returned to the code 72, looking at it upside down and sideways but it told me nothing. I did the same for 6656, which I already knew to be Nolo Serrano. These particular numbers didn't resemble letters, but they might represent letters. It was all too possible that Patricia was setting up a meeting with Ron Cade or Alfredo Lobato. AL could be drawn with numbers, but RC couldn't. I picked up my phone, cradled it in my hand and looked at the numbers 7 and 2. The 7 square contained the letters PRS and the 2 square held ABC. It wasn't hard to pull RC out of that. Ron Cade. When I looked at 6656 I saw NOLO.

Anna had said that the girls liked to get the guys together and set them off. If Patricia was putting Ron Cade and Nolo Serrano together, it was a deadly combination. If what had initially set these guys off was the death of Juan Padilla, tonight could be the final resolution. It had been building for some time and in a way the climax would be a relief, especially if it revealed what had really happened the night Juan Padilla died. The trouble was that one or all of them could get maimed or killed. I was glad Cheyanne was tucked away in the D Home tonight, and I wished that Patricia were there, too.

The phone was already in my hand, so I dialed Anthony Saia's home number and got the message, "If you talk now, I'll listen later."

The message I left on his machine was, "This is Neil. There is going to be trouble at eleven tonight on the Main Canal near Lupe Circle, Lane or Court."

Then I dialed Saia's beeper number, wondering if he used vibrator mode or sound. I got his voice telling me to key in my message. I left my home number and waited a few minutes, but he didn't call back. Either he'd turned the beeper off or he wasn't wearing it. I wondered for a minute exactly where Saia was and what he was doing.

Next I tried the APD, but none of the detectives I'd worked with—Donaldson, Jessup or Mares—were on duty. The dispatcher who took my information gave the distinct impression that she was overworked and underpaid and was putting my information at the bottom of a long list of Saturday-night trouble spots.

I called Patricia's home number, but there was no

answer and no answering machine. This family communicated by beeper. I thought about sending her beeper the message to stay home, but I didn't know how to do it and I doubted she'd listen.

I went into my bedroom and loaded my thirty-eight. Then I put the gun, the map and the beeper in my car and drove to the Kid's shop, where he'd been working late. He'd already put the hood over the parrot's cage and was getting ready to lock up and come home.

I called up the messages I'd found on the beeper's screen and showed them to him. "I think this means Patricia is setting up a meeting on the Main Canal with Ron Cade and Nolo Serrano at eleven," I said.

"How do you get that?" he asked.

I demonstrated how I'd reached my conclusion, but he was dubious. "I don't know, chiquita. Even if you are right, the Main Canal is many miles long."

"Yeah, but I think the meeting will be near Lupe Circle, Lupe Lane or Lupe Court where the ditch forks. I can't get Saia. The APD isn't interested. Somebody has to go," I said. "Do you want to come with me?"

"*Cómo no?*" Why not?

"It could be dangerous."

He shrugged. He wouldn't admit it, but he liked

danger almost as much as I did. My attraction to danger wasn't a problem as long as I took him along.

"I'm bringing my gun," I told him. Usually the Kid wanted nothing to do with guns, but this time we were talking gang.

"*Bueno,*" he said. "*Vamos.*"

21

We started at Lupe Court, the Lupe closest to the shop. If we didn't find anybody there, we intended to work our way south. We had only an hour left and time was of the essence. Lupe Court was a new subdivision off Fourth. A developer had drawn a line through the middle of an alfalfa field, paved it, ended it in a cul-de-sac and sold off the land on either side as building lots. There was a magnificent view of the Sandias, and it was a place to build a dream house. But one person's dream is another person's nightmare. The houses were two stories tall and featured angled roofs, prominent balconies and three-car garages. Houses in New Mexico ought to be closer to the ground. The indigenous architecture gives the impression that it's risen out of the earth and that when its time is over, it intends to sink back in. The houses in Lupe Court cast a large and awkward shadow.

I drove to the end of the cul-de-sac where the lots hadn't been developed yet. Any houses constructed here would have to be even bigger than the others to see over the roofs to the view. There were no cars parked in the cul-de-sac or beside the road. It didn't feel like the right place to me, but since we were here we followed a path that led from the cul-de-sac toward the ditch and ended at a metal fence. There was a gate, but the gate was locked tight to keep people like Patricia, Nolo and Ron Cade out of Lupe Court. We might have found some way around the fence, but time was ticking.

"If this was where they were meeting, someone's car would be parked here," I told the Kid.

He agreed, and we got back in the Nissan and headed south to Lupe Lane, a dirt road that maintained the Valley's rural character, although just north of it was Casa, a home supply store with a large, well-lit parking lot. We cruised through the lot, where several cars were parked, although none that I recognized. Then we drove down Lupe Lane past an adobe house and a vegetable garden with dried stalks of corn high enough to hide a crop of marijuana plants. Lupe Lane got rougher and rockier until it ended in a bump at the ditch bank. There were no cars parked here either, although someone could have walked over from Casa easily enough. We climbed up the ditch bank and walked north toward the place where the Main Canal forked. We didn't have to walk far to see the V because the ditch was lit by the security lights that protected Casa's storage lot. The lot was fenced and circled by razor wire. A large black dog ran down the length of the fence snarling at us. This wasn't the place, either. Too well lit, too well protected.

I looked at the clock when we got back to the car—twenty-five minutes left. Patricia's house was between here and our last stop, Lupe Circle. Just for the heck of it I drove by and stopped outside the chain-link fence. The house was dark. The security lights were on. I beeped my horn, hoping for some reaction, but all I got was a sleepy chow crawling out of its hole and growling at me.

"Usually there are two dogs here," I said to the Kid.

"Maybe she took one with her."

We continued south on Fourth to Lupe Circle. Every Lupe we went to represented a different period in the Valley's development. This street looked like the 1970s to me. The houses were medium-sized and low. The trees were large and well established. There were cars parked in the driveways and beside the street. I cruised Lupe slowly until we neared the place where the circle turned back toward Fourth. My headlights landed on a red and white Fast Five Chevy parked in the loop.

"That's Nolo's car," the Kid said.

I turned my headlights off, backed up and parked about halfway around the circle. We stepped out of the Nissan, shutting the doors behind us very carefully and quietly. We walked in the middle of the road so as not to crunch the gravel on the shoulder and set off all the dogs in the hood. The dogs heard us anyway and began barking one after another, knocking down quiet like dominoes. *"Callensen, perritos,"* whispered the Kid. After they'd had their say the dogs calmed down again. Barking was background music in the Valley anyway. It happened too often to rattle anyone's nerves.

The moon was high and bright enough to illuminate the footpath beside the Main Canal and reflect off the water in the ditch. Up ahead we saw a footbridge with a small waterfall flowing underneath it. The noise of the falling water concealed the sound of our footsteps. Something small and dark scooted across the grating of the bridge and darted into the brush.

"We need to get off the path and walk close to the trees," the Kid whispered.

"Okay," I whispered back, but it was tough going once we left the path. The trees were large cottonwoods with rough-textured bark and branches that reached across the ditch. If we'd been squirrels we could have gotten to our destination by leaping from branch to branch. We would have had a bird's-eye view, and we would have gotten there a lot faster. On the ground it was hard to tell what was substance and what was shadow. We had to get through the weeds and brush without making too much noise and around the obstacles and fences without taking too much time. We'd had fifteen minutes by the car clock when we'd parked. The gentle lapping of the ditch was hiding our more subtle sounds, but then I stepped on a twig, which gave a loud *snap*. It set my heart thumping so hard I thought it would wake the closest household a hundred feet away. We waited for a reaction, but all we heard was the ditch water flowing, an owl hooting, a dog howling.

We started up again, trudging through the underbrush. The waning moon was a scimitar in the sky. Lamplight glowed from the windows of the closest house, saying, In here is warmth and safety, out there lies darkness, La Llorona and the creatures of the night. Ahead of us I could see where the ditch forked and formed a V. The Kid grabbed my arm and pulled me deeper into the shadows.

"What?" I asked.

"*Oye,*" he whispered. Listen.

I didn't hear anything at first but the rippling water. Crying was on my mind, but it was laughter that lifted and separated from the sound of the water. It was a girl's laugh, soft but chilling as ice water dripping on the back of my neck.

A guy answered from the other side of the ditch. The lateral was taking some of the water away, but the action seemed to be taking place on the Main Canal. The guy's voice was rougher than the sound of the water. "Where are you?" he called.

"Over here." The girl's voice came from behind a cottonwood on our side of the ditch.

"Come across the bridge," the guy said

"You come here."

"Are you alone?"

"All alone."

"How do I know I can trust you?" he asked.

"You can." Her laughter this time was an entice-ment. This girl was feeling and enjoying her power.

The guy tried hard to resist. "How do I know you're not packing?" This could be the mating call of the nineties.

"Trust me. Come on over."

"Prove it."

"Ooookay." A small pistol—probably a twenty-two—flew out from behind the girl's tree and flopped into the water like a silver fish.

"I'm comin'," the guy said.

He hadn't said whether he was packing and the girl hadn't asked. The Kid tensed beside me. My own hand gripped my thirty-eight. The guy stepped out of the shadows and onto the footbridge. His feet scraped the grate. His hands gripped the railing. The bridge swayed under his weight. He was a vain and pretty boy, a boy who'd have to prove himself over and over again. His baggy clothes and turned-backward hat gave him a wide and distinctive silhouette. In the moonlight it made him into a target that was nearly impossible to miss.

The girl's laugh turned derisive. "Take your breath away, Nolo," she said.

"Get down," I yelled.

The only cover lay beneath Nolo in the ditch, but he didn't take it. He looked into the water. It was only a second, but it was too long. His hand went into his pants reaching for his piece.

"Get down now," I screamed.

Semiautomatic fire started and repeated until the clip ran out. The Kid and I pressed ourselves hard into the ground. Bullets kicked up the dirt around us. Nolo jerked inside his baggy clothes, crumpled up and fell to the floor of the bridge. We heard the sound of footsteps running down the path. The Kid jumped the ditch and gave chase. I ran to Nolo and held him in my arms, trying hard to find a pulse or a breath. His blood poured out of him and squirted through the grating, turning the ditch water red.

Patricia stepped out from behind the tree holding her chow on a short leash. She looked at Nolo with the hardest eyes I'd ever seen. *"Muerto,"* she said.

There wasn't any life left in Nolo, and I laid him gently down.

"How did you find us here?" she asked.

I saw her beeper attached to her belt, but my response was, "I can't say."

"Was it Cheyanne?" She tightened her grip on the leash. If Cheyanne had confided in me, Patricia would consider that a betrayal and a betrayal in this world could end your life.

"No."

She cut the dog a little slack. "Nolo's the one who beat her, you know. He cut her face. He made her confess. She saw Nolo shoot Juan, and he didn't want her out on the street telling anybody. He was afraid the other Four O's would find out and off him."

"Why did he kill Juan?"

"It was a dis. Juan laughed at him and told him he was too pretty. Nolo wanted to be a leader and make his name come out."

"But first Nolo tried to put the blame on Ron Cade?"

"Juan hated Cade, so the Four O's and the police were ready to believe he killed Juan until he got his alibi. When Nolo heard that he made Cheyanne say she did it. It wouldn't matter what happened to her—she's only thirteen years old."

"Is that what got Alfredo Lobato into the gang? Acting as a witness against Cade?"

"Yeah. Nolo got him in. He was Alfredo's hero. Alfredo would do anything for him. Word got around that Cheyanne had been at the killing. When you saw Ron and Cheyanne together that time he was trying to get her to tell him who'd put the hit out on him."

"What was she doing at the strip mall that night?" I asked.

"She went to tell Juan to stop trying to rank in her brother. Nolo and Alfredo came up. She saw it all happen and she picked up the bullet, but it wasn't her fault. She was in the wrong place."

"Ron Cade was the shooter this time?"

"You got it."

"You shouldn't have gotten involved, Patricia."

"Nobody else was doin' nothin'. Nolo had it coming," she answered.

As Anna had said, the girls were more than willing to play their parts. And as Saia had said, gang justice was swift, brutal and effective. But it might as well be happening on the screen as far as they were concerned. Death and violence meant nothing to them. Patricia stood before me as still and indifferent as a statue.

Cade hadn't gotten far. I heard the sound of fighting and swearing in the brush and ran across the bridge to see who'd come out on top. I had my thirty-eight but I didn't have to use it because the Kid was coming down the moonlit path pushing Ron Cade in front of him. Cade's shirt had been yanked up over his head, pulled behind his back and knotted, exposing his pale and scrawny tattooed chest. The shirt held his hands behind him, but his mouth was free and screaming abuse. "Fucking wetback," he yelled. "Get your dirty hands off of me."

"Shut up." The Kid gave him a shove.

I handed over the thirty-eight. The Kid hated guns, but Cade didn't know that. The Kid sat Cade down on the path and stood over him, aiming the pistol at his head. Cade gave him an evil stare, but he kept his mouth shut. Up close he looked like his pictures, but paler and meaner. His eyes were burning with anger. His mouth was a dark hole.

"He's dead?" The Kid nodded in Nolo's direction.

"Yeah."

"Where's the girl?"

I turned around, but Patricia and her chow had disappeared into the trees and gone back whatever way they'd come. "*Se fue*," I said. "She's gone."

Lights began spinning in the area south of us

where Lupe Circle met the ditch. Either Saia had gotten my message or the APD was finally responding to my call or someone had heard the gunshots and called the police. The cops ran down the path, crisscrossing the night with their flashlights.

"Everybody freeze," one of them yelled.

At this point freezing came easy enough for me. Nolo wasn't going anywhere, and the Kid had Ron Cade locked in place. One cop went to Nolo, two went to the Kid and Cade, the fourth one came over to me. I guess I looked like the oldest and most responsible citizen. My cop asked me what had happened.

"We were out for a walk," I said. "We saw that guy"—I pointed to Nolo—"crossing the bridge. Then the one sitting over there on the ground shot him with a semiautomatic. My boyfriend chased the shooter. You'll probably find the murder weapon somewhere near where he brought him down." The Kid's eyebrows might have been rising at this version of events, but he didn't contradict me.

It was obvious that Cade was a gang member, but the cops weren't treating the Kid with any respect, either. He was young. He was Hispanic. On the other hand, so were two of the cops.

The second cop eyed the Kid suspiciously and barked, "Drop the weapon." The Kid did as he was told.

"Who does the gun belong to?" the cop asked.

"It's registered to me," I said.

"Why were you out here with a pistol?" my cop asked.

"Would you take a walk along the ditch at night without one?"

"I wouldn't take a walk on the ditch at night at all," the cop said. "What were you doing out here?"

"Getting some air."

The casing from Cade's semiautomatic lay on the path, clearly visible in the glare from the flashlights. Nolo's cop got on his radio and called for an ambulance, although it was too late to do Nolo any good. The Kid and his cop walked back to the spot where Cade had fallen and found the murder weapon lying in the brush.

"Were there any other witnesses?" my cop asked me.

I hesitated briefly, then said, "No." It was a lawyer's instinct not to give anybody up. There was no way of proving Patricia had been here unless she confessed.

Cade's cop read him his rights. Cade had been through this before and he knew the drill. "I want my lawyer," he said.

The cops asked the Kid and me to come in and give statements. When we left the scene they were already putting the yellow police tape up.

★   ★   ★

The statements the Kid and I gave at the police station were nearly identical, and they both omitted any mention of Patricia. But when we got home he asked me why I hadn't told the police about her. "She got that boy killed," he said.

Patricia had been an accessory. There was no doubt about that. "Nolo killed Juan Padilla, assaulted Cheyanne and let her take the rap for him. In Patricia's mind, justice has been served."

But not in the Kid's mind. "She could do it again."

"I don't know that two years in the Girls' School would change that," I said. I'd let my client do time for a crime she hadn't committed. I wasn't sure I had the heart to put another young girl in detention. "It would be hard to prove that she was involved."

"What about the beeper?"

"I checked it. A bunch of new messages came in and erased the ones she'd received from Cade and Nolo."

"You didn't lock them in?"

"I only have one lock-in space. I reserved it for Nolo's message to Cheyanne."

"Maybe Cade will tell on her." Obviously the Kid didn't think justice had been served, but he didn't seem to want it bad enough to go back to the police.

"Maybe." In a way I hoped Cade would tell; it would get my conscience off the hook, because Patricia had killed Nolo just as surely as if she'd pulled the trigger. There was no question of self-defense. The murder had been as cold and calculated as they come, and the motive had been revenge.

"Now you know what happened, can you get Cheyanne out of the D Home?" the Kid asked.

"I don't know. Everything Patricia told me is hearsay. The fact that Cade shot Nolo doesn't prove Nolo killed Juan Padilla. It would help if Alfredo Lobato told the truth or the police came up with a weapon."

After that the Kid went to bed. I took off my clothes, which were caked stiff with Nolo Serrano's blood, put them in a black plastic bag and dumped it in the garbage pail. I showered and washed my hair, watching Nolo's blood run down the drain. No matter what color they carry, they all bleed red. Then I went to bed, where in spite of—or maybe because of—the events of that night, I slept a deep and dreamless sleep. I'd already had a nightmare with my eyes open wide.

22

In the morning Saia called me. "I got your message last night," he said. "I hear that by the time the police arrived the crime had been committed."

"Did they respond to your call or mine?"

"Mine."

"What took them so long?" The APD had the capacity to go to all three sites concurrently, but I'd had to do it consecutively.

"I wasn't able to get the message to them immediately."

"Turned off your pager, had you?"

"For a while."

"Where was it? Hanging from the bedpost?"

"I was with Jennifer." He cleared his throat and changed the subject. "I have a police report here that says you and your friend were walking along the Main Canal and happened to witness Ron Cade shooting Nolo Serrano."

"That's right."

"You knew there was going to be trouble. Are you going to reveal your source?"

"Let's just say I happened to be eavesdropping on the information highway. The minute I got the information I tried to pass it on to you. It's not my fault you weren't in receiving mode."

He coughed and cleared his throat again.

"You got Ron Cade. You can't be complaining about that," I said.

"I'm not. I have a weapon. I've got you and your friend for witnesses. What I'm lacking is motive. Or is the fact that these guys were armed and dangerous gangbangers motive enough?"

"The word I got is that Nolo Serrano killed Juan Padilla, then told his fellow gang members that Cade had been the shooter. It put Cade's life in jeopardy. This shooting was in retaliation."

"How do you explain that Cade's alibi for the night Padilla was killed turned out to be worthless?"

"He was engaged in some other crime?"

"Always a possibility. Can you prove that Nolo was the shooter in the Padilla case?"

"No, but I did hear that your witness lied to cover for Nolo. He was a Four O wannabe and Nolo promised to get him in. Your witness is now wearing the mourning shirt of a Four O member." Fortunately Saia didn't ask me how I'd gotten that information.

"We'll bring him in for further questioning."

"Good."

"You do know that a witness who changes his story lacks credibility."

So did a witness with a vested interest, which included me. My hope was that Saia would see the wisdom of a plea bargain and not take this case to trial. He wouldn't get everything he wanted, but Cade would do time. "I know."

"Can you get your client to recant now that Nolo is dead?"

"I'll try."

"I suppose it was fear of him that put her in the D Home in the first place."

"It was a determining factor. He was the one who cut her face."

"Why did Serrano pick her?"

"She was at the scene of the crime. The Four O's were trying to rank in her half brother, Danny Ortega."

"Leo's son?"

"Right. Cheyanne went to tell Juan Padilla to leave Danny alone and she witnessed a shooting."

"What caused it? Some sort of intramural rivalry?"

"That and a dis. Nolo wanted to be a leader."

"Now that the gangs are the size of corporations, fighting inside them has become as big a problem as fighting between them. It's amazing what they'll do over an insult."

"They don't have a very high opinion of themselves, Anthony. Add hormones, drugs and guns. It's a bad combination. You were wrong about Leo, you know. He's been a good father to Danny."

"Maybe it's time to get out of the prosecuting business. I was wrong about Serrano, too. I thought that kid had potential."

"Me too. He bled out in my arms."

"That's a tough one. I'll give you a call after we talk to Cade and my witness. See what you can do with your client."

"Will do."

He had one last question. "Did you ever really believe she was guilty?"

"I didn't know. I will say that representing her was the hardest thing I've ever done."

"I can understand that," Saia said.

*　　　*　　　*

My client had been in the D Home long enough for it to have lost some charm. Her own home was looking better to her and the outside less dangerous now that Nolo Serrano was off the street. True to his word, he had protected her while she was in detention. She wasn't quite ready to recant, however, unless Alfredo Lobato changed his testimony. Until it was proven that Nolo had killed Juan, she considered the Four O's a threat.

But Lobato stuck to his story that Cade had been the shooter. Nolo seemed to have a hold over him from beyond the grave. True to Cade's reputation as a sleaze, he and his lawyer not only implicated Patricia, they tried to blame her. It strained credibility that a hard-core gangbanger had been forced to kill another gangbanger by a fourteen-year-old girl, even one as hard as Patricia. When the police brought her in for questioning, she was accompanied by her parents, not her lawyer. The detectives were tough and thorough. Patricia's parents demanded answers. She broke down and admitted her part in the shooting of Nolo Serrano. She would soon turn fifteen, the age when she could drive and be prosecuted as an adult, but she hadn't crossed that line yet. All Saia could get was two years in the Girls' School. He was inclined to leniency toward Patricia, since her testimony helped him convince Ron Cade to plead out. But Patricia's parents were repelled by their daughter's acts, and they wanted her to do the time. Saia recommended a counselor who had a good record working with teens in trouble and their parents. It offered some hope that Patricia would come out of the Girls' School with a better set of values than when she went in.

A few days after the shooting I was standing in the kitchen trying to figure out what to do about dinner. The cupboard was bare, and I was leaning toward Casa de Benavidez. The doorbell rang. I went out-side, opened the chevron door and found Danny standing on the other side holding his bike. He had a new hairdo, shaved clean around the sides with a skullcap left on top.

"What do you call that one?" I asked.

"The buzz. My dad did it with his electric razor."

"Cool," I said .

"Will my sister go free now that Nolo is dead?"

"I hope so."

"Do you have a plastic bag I could borrow?"

"You're not planning to put it over somebody's head, are you?"

"Nope. It has to be about this big." He made motions with his hands about a foot square.

"I'll see what I can do." I went into the house and came back with a brand-new plastic bag approxi-mately the designated size.

He folded the bag up and put it in his pocket. "Can you come with me?"

"Okay."

He pedaled away with his head down and his elbows poking into the street. When he got to the ditch he turned north. I followed him down the footpath, studying the patterns his tires made in the dirt. I watched him cross Montera and Lujan way ahead of me, but when he got to his destination he stopped and waited for me to catch up. He stood next to a valve that controlled the flow of water into a narrow field. The adjacent field was lush and green. Horses and a long-legged colt ran up and down it, churning up the soil. But this field was full of dead weeds and beyond dry. A horse wouldn't leave a nick in this hard ground. It was one of those fields that no longer used its life-giving connection to the ditch.

Sunflowers bobbed along the ditch bank in a wind-driven dance. The Sandias were a remote and distant blue. Behind the unused valve was a wooden backboard. Danny reached into it, parted the weeds and showed me a thirty-eight revolver.

"Whew," I said. "When did you find it?"

"Last week. I knew it would be near the ditch. After Juan was killed I rode my bike up and down here every day looking for it."

"Don't blame yourself. I saw the policeman go right by this spot and he didn't find it, either."

"Do you think it's the gun that killed Juan?"

"There's a good chance. Why didn't you tell me sooner?"

"I was afraid. But now . . ." He took out the plastic bag, folded it over his hand and reached down to pick up the pistol. He knew the evidence procedure; he'd probably seen it often enough on TV.

"Don't do that, Danny," I said. "It would be better if the police find it in place. Will you stay here and watch it while I call them?"

"Okay," he said. He'd been a good guardian so far; I felt I could trust him.

But I couldn't help acting like an adult. "Don't touch it," I warned.

The Kid's shop wasn't far and I ran over there to call Detective Jessup. The Kid could tell just by looking at me that something positive had happened.

"*Qué pasa?*" he asked.

"I think Danny found Nolo's gun."

"*Bueno!*" said the Kid.

"*Bueno,*" echoed the parrot, picking up on the excitement in the Kid's voice and raising its vocabulary level a notch. The bird liked its new word so much that it repeated it over and over again.

"That's what's been wrong with Mimo," I said.

"What?"

"There hasn't been enough excitement around here."

"*Bueno*," said the bird.

Detective Jessup was excited herself when I told her the news, but since she was a cop, it had to be a controlled excitement.

"What makes you think it's Serrano's gun?" she asked.

"He had to get rid of it somewhere. It's the right weapon in the right place."

"I'm on my way over," she said.

The Kid went back to work. I went back to the valve, sat down on the ditch bank and waited with Danny for Jessup to show up.

"Now do you think my sister will go free?" he asked me.

"We'll see. It can be hard to get fingerprints from a gun."

But this gun had been sheltered. Nolo Serrano's prints were on file and they matched the only print the crime lab was able to get from the gun. With the bullet Cheyanne had turned in, the crime lab had no trouble ascertaining that Nolo Serrano had fired the gun that killed Juan Padilla.

The day Cheyanne was released from the D Home I waited outside for her with her family.

"Hey, bro," she said, running her hand across Danny's skullcap. "Cool do."

Danny laughed and kicked up some dirt.

"I'm real glad you're coming home," Sonia said, hugging her daughter.

"Me too," Cheyanne replied.

Leo and Cheyanne gave each other a tenuous hug. At least they were trying. "I'm real proud of you guys, you know that?" Leo said. "You proved you can do it."

"Do what?" asked Danny.

"Beat the gangs," Leo said.

Cheyanne came over to me and we faced each other. What kind of a relationship would this be now anyway? I wondered. I wasn't her mother. She wouldn't be needing a lawyer anymore. I was too old to be her friend. I extended my hand and she took it, but I didn't know if I'd be seeing her again.

A few weeks later the doorbell rang. I couldn't see anyone through the chevron pattern, but I opened the door anyway and found a baby lying on the stoop. It was wrapped in a blanket and tucked inside one of those plastic baby carriers with a handle. I bent over for a closer look and the baby started to cry. I was considering picking it up when Cheyanne laughed, came around the corner of the courtyard, flipped the doll over and turned it off. She was wearing her extra-large Chicago Bulls t-shirt. Her fingernails were painted blue. Her blonde curls bobbed around her head, but they didn't hide all the scars. There was a jagged red lightning mark on one side of her face. It didn't destroy her looks, but it gave them another dimension. Tabatoe was with her, and the cat turned and raced down the driveway, heading for my catnip patch.

"How are you doing?" I asked Cheyanne.

"Pretty good."

"You didn't steal a doll from the school again, did you?"

"No. It was my turn to take it home. It goes back tomorrow. Would you mind if I, um . . ."

"Got on the computer?"

"Right."

"Come on in."

Cheyanne followed me across the courtyard and into the living room. She put the doll on the sofa and sat down at the computer. Before she began searching for fine guys on the Internet, I asked her about Patricia.

"She's in the D Home until she gets sentenced. I talk to her a lot."

"She's going to end up in the Girls' School, you know."

"I know. It'll be hard for her in there. Nolo's homegirls are already hassling her. She doesn't care what she looks like anymore. She orders pizza all the time and is getting fat."

Weight gain was a place girls went to hide out from guys and life and death. "Is she talking to her parents?"

"Yeah, they talk, and her mother goes to see her. Patricia told me that when Nolo died she thought that meant he couldn't do nothin' to hurt us anymore. But now she feels she can't get rid of him."

"He's hanging from her neck like a rotting animal."

"How did you know? That's the way I felt when I was in the D Home. I didn't kill Juan Padilla, but I had to act like I did. I tried to pretend what that would be like and I felt I was responsible for him twenty-four–seven. I hated the way his women looked at me in the courtroom."

"Did you tell Patricia that?"

"Yeah, but she didn't listen. She wanted to make Nolo pay for what he did."

Payback was one form of justice that had existed for a long, long time. "We all pay, don't we?"

"I know that now."

I hadn't seen the gray cat for a while, and I asked Cheyanne if she knew what had become of it.

"Leo got tired of it hanging around, punking Tabatoe and stealing her food, and he trapped it."

"Did he kill it?"

"No. He took it to the animal shelter."

Maybe the time had come for it to be somebody

else's dark shadow. "How are you getting along with your mother and Leo?"

"Better." Her fingers were itching for the keyboard. "Can I?"

"Sure."

I'd been expecting her to get on the Internet and Teen Chat, but she opened Digital Schoolhouse instead and inserted a disc in the CD-ROM drive. A spiderweb appeared on the screen. In a tinny voice, "Itsy-Bitsy Spider" began to play and Cheyanne sang along. Her fingers left the keyboard and climbed the waterspout.

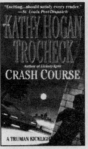